For more than forty years,
Yearling has been the leading name
in classic and award-winning literature
for young readers.

Yearling books feature children's
favorite authors and characters,
providing dynamic stories of adventure,
humor, history, mystery, and fantasy.

Trust Yearling paperbacks to entertain,
inspire, and promote the love of reading
in all children.

THE WHITE GATES

BONNIE RAMTHUN

A YEARLING BOOK

All rights reserved. Published in the United States by Yearling, an imprint of Random House Children's Books, a division of Random House, Inc., New York. Originally published in hardcover in the United States by Random House Children's Books, a division of Random House, Inc., in 2008.

Yearling and the jumping horse design are registered trademarks of Random House, Inc.

Visit us on the Web! www.randomhouse.com/kids

Educators and librarians, for a variety of teaching tools, visit us at www.randomhouse.com/teachers

The Library of Congress has cataloged the hardcover edition of this work as follows:
Ramthun, Bonnie.
The White Gates / by Bonnie Ramthun.
Summary: When his mother becomes the doctor in Snow Park, Colorado, twelve-year-old Tor learns of a curse placed on the town's doctors many years before by an eccentric Ute woman, but suspects that a modern-day villain is hiding behind that curse.
ISBN: 978-0-375-84554-3 (trade) — ISBN: 978-0-375-94554-0 (lib. bdg.) — ISBN: 978-0-375-84555-0 (pbk.) — ISBN: 978-0-375-89232-5 (e-book)
[1. Blessing and cursing—Fiction. 2. Snowboarding—Fiction. 3. Physicians—Fiction. 4. Mothers and sons—Fiction. 5. Schools—Fiction. 6. Moving, Household—Fiction. 7. Ute Indians—Fiction. 8. Indians of North America—Colorado—Fiction. 9. Colorado—Fiction. 10. Mystery and detective stories.] I. Title.
PZ7.R1485Whi 2008   [Fic]—dc22   2007012800

Printed in the United States of America
10 9 8 7 6 5 4 3 2 1
First Yearling Edition

THIS NOVEL IS DEDICATED TO TOM SIMON.
HE MAKES A SNOWBOARD SING.

CONTENTS

THE WHITE GATES

1 ☠ FLIGHT FOR LIFE

TOR WAS AWAKE the moment the door to his room opened.

"Torin?"

"I'm up, Mom," he said, sitting up in bed.

His mother came into the room and turned on the light. Tor squinted. The room was full of boxes, some open, some still taped shut. Tor had been too tired to do much more than throw some blankets on his bed last night. He hadn't even unpacked his books or his CDs.

"I have to go into the clinic. Now. I don't want to leave you alone, so I need you to come with me," his mother said. She started rummaging in the closet. "Where's your snowsuit?"

"My snowsuit?" Tor asked, and for a moment wondered if he wasn't as awake as he thought. Weren't snowsuits for little kids? He was twelve years old, not six.

"Overalls, coveralls—what are they called around here?" his mom said, frantically throwing clothing out of the closet. "We have to go, Tor. Now. There's a boy at the clinic and I need to get there right now—there!"

Tor scrambled out of bed and grabbed the ridiculous blue snowsuit his mom was holding out to him. Somebody needed his mom's help. He hadn't gotten used to thinking of her as a doctor after all those years she'd spent in school and in training. But she was a doctor at last, and someone needed her.

He pulled the blue suit over his pajama bottoms and T-shirt. His pj's were printed with blue waves and tiny California surfers. Yesterday he'd been a California kid. He stuffed his feet into the brand-new snow boots his mom had bought. *Zip* went the suit. Done. He flipped the attached hood forward and looked at his mom, who was dressed in a similar suit. Hers was red. He and his mom looked like two characters from a really lame Saturday-morning cartoon. He wanted to say what he was thinking, but his mom's face was too serious, almost scared. He said nothing.

"Follow me," his mom said, and Tor clumped after her.

When Tor followed his mother outside, his lungs instantly stopped working. His breath froze. He started coughing. This was like outer space. The air felt like knives going into his lungs. There was a tiny crackling sound as all the moisture in his nose froze. That was so gross. Tor didn't want to imagine frozen snot, but too late, he did.

His fingers started tingling, and he shoved them into his pockets. Huge puffs of vapor came out in a cloud around his mother's head as she pulled the door shut behind them and locked it. Tor looked at his new hometown. He'd seen it for the first time that afternoon when they'd driven in. Crowds of skiers and shoppers had filled the streets. Now it was late at night and Snow Park was silent.

He looked up and down the streets and saw only a single set of tire tracks in the powdery snow. Streetlights on every block cast down pale circles, but no one walked on the sidewalks and no lights shone in the buildings. Tor's new house was a block off the main street of Snow Park and stood near the top of a small hill. The streets below him were decorated for the Christmas tourist season, and green wreaths and red ribbons decorated every storefront.

Snow Park could be a miniature town inside an enormous snow globe. Tor almost expected to see a department store dummy standing at the corner holding a fake pile of Christmas boxes. This vision was so instantly creepy he shivered.

"This way," his mom said, starting down the sidewalk. Tor followed, glancing back at the garage where the car was parked. His mom saw the look, or somehow knew what Tor was thinking. "The car would take longer to start than we have time," she said. "We'll be at the clinic in just a minute. It's only two blocks. Can you breathe okay? Put your glove over your face—oh, I'm sorry. No gloves yet. Try to breathe through your jacket collar. It must be twenty below out here."

"I'm good," Tor said. He wasn't going to complain. He hadn't thought that breathing might be a problem, though. He tucked his chin into the warmth of his snowsuit. The snow was so cold it didn't crunch. It squeaked like Styrofoam under his feet. Tor tried to ignore the cold as they hurried down the street.

"Dr. Sinclair!" someone yelled.

"Here," Tor's mom called. Tor raised his eyes and saw the Snow Park Medical Clinic. The building was small and had a deep porch and a steeply pitched roof. The windows were now brightly lighted. There were two cars parked outside the clinic, and as Tor looked, two more cars turned a corner and headed toward the clinic, their tailpipes sending plumes of exhaust into the cold air. Another car turned the corner from the other direction and crunched down the street. Whatever was going on, a lot of people apparently knew about it.

"Doctor," someone said, startling Tor. He hadn't seen the man standing in the darkness of the porch. His voice was thin and high and anxious. "Thank you for coming."

"Of course," Dr. Sinclair said.

Tor followed his mother up the steps. The man was now gripping his mom's arm, his fingers disappearing into the fabric of her snowsuit, dragging her inside the clinic. Tor followed his mom, still looking down to keep his face deep in his hood. In the warmth of the clinic his nose and cheeks started tingling and stinging. He drew a deep breath and was grateful it no longer burned his lungs.

There was someone lying on the floor, wrapped up in a blanket. A man knelt at his side. Tor peered, trying to see.

Suddenly the door burst open behind them and Tor turned to see two teenagers, both wearing identical blue coats, their eyes wide and frightened.

"What's going on?" one of the boys said. "Coach?"

"Excuse me," Tor's mom commanded, and the room hushed instantly. Dr. Susan Sinclair's curly brown hair stood out from her head and her nose was red from the cold. She wasn't tall, and she was slender, but there was no doubt that she was in charge.

Tor's dad hadn't wanted his mom to go to medical school, all those years ago. Tor wasn't sure why, exactly. He thought sometimes that his dad hadn't wanted his mom spending all that time away from him. Or maybe he really didn't think she could do it. Tor's dad had told his mom that she couldn't get into medical school because the exams were too hard. But she had taken the pre-med courses one by one, studying nights and weekends, and she'd passed them. Then he'd told her that medical schools wanted young people, not moms with

5

kids. But she'd applied and was accepted. Then he'd told her she was too little and frail for all the tough things that doctors had to do—crack chests, give CPR, and deliver babies.

Tor's dad had gotten a little desperate at the end, but nothing worked. She'd left them, finally, both Tor and his dad, and his parents had divorced. Now, six years later, she looked every inch the doctor she'd wanted to be. Tor wished his dad could have seen his mom the way she was now, back then. Maybe things would have turned out differently.

"Everyone out except relatives," Dr. Sinclair ordered. "Tor, I need you to sit over there." She pointed at a chair in the far corner, and Tor nodded. He knew his mom needed to work on the boy who was lying on the floor, and he felt strange that she was the person everyone was looking to for help. He sat down.

The two blue-coated teenagers turned for the door. One of them looked at Tor with an expression that Tor couldn't figure out for a moment. Then he got it. The boy was glaring at him with complete and utter hatred.

"It's the curse," the boy spat. The other teenager saw Tor's expression and he grabbed his friend's arm.

"Shut up!" he hissed, and they hurried from the room.

Tor turned back to his mom to ask her what the boy meant, but she was busy. She had snapped on surgical gloves and had turned to the sick boy—a teenager, really—on the floor. Tor saw the frothy pink blood coming out of the teenager's mouth and nose. The boy was gasping, and pink bubbles came out his nose every time he drew hoarse breath.

This was the first time Tor had seen something like that, and he wondered if he was going to get sick like people did in movies. Evidently, he wasn't like those people, because he didn't feel sick at all. He was, instead, powerfully interested. The blood was pink, not the dark red of a nosebleed, and it was full of bubbles. Why was that?

"You're his father?" his mom said to the man who knelt by the boy. She'd finished a quick examination and now she expertly slipped a mask on the boy's face and turned a knob on a green tank. There was a loud hiss like an angry snake and then a steady hissing sound after that.

"Yes," the man replied. "I'm Dempsy Slader." Mr. Slader was wringing his hands, his face twisted in anguish.

"I'm Coach Rollins," said the man who had led Tor's mom into the clinic. The coach looked calm, but a muscle jumped under his eye and his skin was so pale Tor thought of a fish he'd once seen washed up on the beach, long dead.

"My son," Mr. Slader continued, "he got back late from a strategy meeting for the snowboarding team. Later, after he went to bed, I heard him coughing and it didn't sound right, it sounded horrible. Then there was the blood. I called Coach Rollins, but he said nothing had happened at the meeting. He didn't know what was going on either—"

"We called you, and then we brought him here," the coach said.

"His name?" Dr. Sinclair asked.

"Brian. Brian Slader."

"Brian, listen to me," Dr. Sinclair said, turning to the boy on the floor. "You've got a bit of pulmonary edema in your lungs and we have to get you to a lower elevation right away. You're not poisoned, you don't have a disease, but we do have to call a Flight for Life helicopter right now. Nod if you understand me."

Tor saw the bloody boy nod, very slowly. Dr. Sinclair squeezed his arm kindly.

"Don't try to talk," she said. "This oxygen mask is going to give you some good air and you need to keep it on. That's going to help you breathe."

Tor watched as his mother pressed her fingers to Brian's wrist. She had a stethoscope around her neck and she took it and listened to his chest. Her face didn't change expression, and Tor thought that was probably not a good thing.

"You need to call a Flight for Life helicopter?" Mr. Slader said. He looked paler and even more frightened than before. "You said—he's going to be okay?"

"I think so, yes, but we need to get him down to a

lower elevation immediately," Dr. Sinclair said smoothly. "If you don't have insurance—"

"No, it's not that," Mr. Slader said. "I'm just—a *helicopter*?"

"Your son is seriously ill," Dr. Sinclair said. She had taken out a cell phone and dialed a number, and now she raised the phone to her ear.

Tor looked out the clinic window at the shapes in frost-cloaked car windows. The two teenagers had gotten into one of the waiting cars but they hadn't driven off—the cars just sat there, the exhaust plumes from their running engines sending white clouds into the black sky. As Tor looked out the window, two more cars drove down the street and nosed into parking spots.

Coach Rollins left the room and went out to speak to one of the teenagers in the cars. He stood up and made a commanding, waving gesture to all the cars that could only mean: Go home. He came back in and put a comforting hand on Mr. Slader's shoulder.

"I'm sorry, Dempsy. We were all together tonight, just a few hours ago, and I wanted to know if something had happened to Brian after we ended the strategy meeting. I called Jeff to see if they'd gone out for burgers after the meeting. Jeff, he must have called everyone else on the team to let them know Brian is sick. That's why they all showed up here. They just want to help."

Mr. Slader nodded but Tor didn't think he'd heard a word Coach Rollins had said.

Dr. Sinclair was already on the phone and Tor could hear part of the conversation. It seemed to be held in a world of doctor-speak, with "stats" and "emergent" thrown in with words like "edema" and "ringers." She hung up and turned to Mr. Slader. "I need you to get a gurney so we can get him off the floor and in some heated blankets. Have we met before, Coach Rollins?"

"Randy Rollins, ma'am. We've met, but I was in my uniform."

"*Deputy* Rollins?" Dr. Sinclair said.

"That's right," he said. "I'm also coach of the high school snowboarding team. Brian's on the team. He was fine tonight. We weren't working out at all, just talking over strategy at our team meeting—"

"Can't we just drive him—" Mr. Slader interrupted, but Dr. Sinclair held up a hand.

"There are two mountain passes between here and Denver," she said. "He needs to get down in altitude *now,* or he's going to be in serious trouble. We can't spare the time to drive."

"Yes, ma'am," Mr. Slader said, sounding like he'd been punched in the stomach.

"Brian here is going to be all right," Dr. Sinclair said, and squeezed the boy's hand. Tor looked at Brian, who was indeed looking better under his oxygen mask. There was still bubbly pink blood coming from his mouth, but his eyes weren't so strange and distant anymore, like he was looking at something nobody else could see.

"I'll get the gurney," Coach Rollins said.

"I need a few minutes to get him an IV and warm up blankets, and we'll get the ambulance to take him to the airfield," Dr. Sinclair said.

She looked over at Tor and, before she could say anything motherly, he immediately spoke up.

"I'm good."

She nodded at him approvingly and turned back to her patient.

When the Flight for Life helicopter came in, collected Brian Slader, and took off, it was the strangest thing Tor had ever seen. The beating helicopter blades swirled powdery snow around until there was nothing but smears of light in a white cloud, some red and green and some pure white, and behind it was the total blackness of night. The blades kept appearing and disappearing in the clouds of snow until they looked like beating wings. Suddenly the wings swept up into the sky and disappeared into the darkness.

Tor sighed and pressed himself closer to the heating vents of Mr. Slader's car. They weren't giving out anything even close to heat, but there was a vague sort of warmth there.

His mom appeared out of the snow, which was settling back down to the ground now that the helicopter had gone. Mr. Slader was with her, along with Coach Rollins.

The car door opened and his mom, looking cold and tired, clambered in. Mr. Slader got in on the driver's side and all the tiny bit of warmth that Tor had managed to build up blew out the doors and was gone. The coach waved a hand at them and walked away.

"You need to drive to Denver to be with him," Dr. Sinclair said. "I'm sorry you couldn't go in the helicopter but they need to be as light as possible to get over the passes."

"My wife is packing right now," Mr. Slader said. "Let me take you home first."

"Put your seat belt on, honey," Dr. Sinclair said to Tor. "I've called on too many people in the ER who didn't wear their seat belts."

"Called?" Tor asked.

"Called, as in, called the time of death," Dr. Sinclair said matter-of-factly. "Put your seat belt on."

Tor put his seat belt on. So did Mr. Slader.

Tor's mom followed him into his room. He stepped out of his boots, stripped off his blue snowsuit, and was deep in the covers before his mom had finished kicking off her own boots. She stood in the doorway and looked at him with a smile that made him feel warm clear through but also embarrassed.

"Thanks for being so good, Tor," his mom said, unzipping her suit. Her stethoscope was still around her neck. She was very slim, and Tor had once thought she was the prettiest mom ever. When she was around, that was—before she decided to leave Tor and his dad and go to medical school.

Tor knew he looked a lot like his mom, except his brown hair didn't curl because he kept it cut short. Their eyes were the same, though—a pale leafy green that looked blue in the sunlight and turned as muddy as swamp water when they got mad. They used to rub noses like Eskimos when Tor was four years old, rub noses and giggle and bat their long brown eyelashes against each other and stare into each other's identical eyes. It seemed like a million years ago.

"I don't mean 'good,' really," she continued, sitting on Tor's bed and taking his hands in hers. "Your hands are like ice!"

"I'm warm," Tor said, although he wasn't yet. His feet were still freezing. Still, he thought he would be soon. The blanket on his new bed was a fluffy down comforter and it had already started to heat him up. There was something inside him that was tightly clenched, like a fist. He hadn't even realized he was tense. His mom was still holding his hands, but she wasn't being gooey about it. She was just holding them.

"Is that guy going to be okay, Mom?" Tor asked.

"I think so, honey. Before I was a doctor, I probably would have said, 'Sure.' But now I'm a doc, and I'm never sure."

"I thought doctors knew everything," Tor said.

"Not everything," his mom said, and her eyes were sad. They weren't exactly talking about Brian Slader anymore. She stood up, giving Tor's hands a squeeze before she let them go. "Before I forget, tomorrow, during clinic, I'm going to send you down to the Pro Shop. They'll get you your gear."

"Gear?"

"Snowboarding gear," Dr. Sinclair said. "Merrill Douglas runs the Pro Shop and he's got a daughter. She's twelve, too. I asked him if he'd set you up with some snowboarding lessons. That is, if you want to. Do you want to?"

"Sure," Tor said, trying not to sound too eager.

"Good, okay," his mom said. She smiled at him. "Maybe you'll meet his daughter and some other kids from school. There's only a few weeks from Thanksgiving to Christmas break, but you'll get a chance to meet your teachers and check out the program up here."

"Sure," Tor said again, much less enthusiastically.

"But first, boarding. The riders I talk to all say snowboarding is like surfing a mountain. I hope you like it." His mom paused. "And I hope you like it here, with me."

She walked back quickly, leaned forward, and smoothed his hair back and kissed his forehead.

"Snowboarding," Tor whispered.

Then he was asleep.

2 ☠ GEARING UP

SNOW PARK IN the daylight was quite different than Snow Park at two o'clock in the morning. The streets of the town were thronged with shoppers and skiers, some still wearing big colorful plastic boots that made them walk like Frankenstein, others in baggy pants and floppy coats and snowboarding boots. Lots of women wore their hair in braids, and everyone was wearing vividly colored winter coats, hats, and gloves.

Many of the shoppers held bags and bundles of early Christmas shopping. The shops were all decorated and they were all open, but the air was cold and the shoppers' breaths puffed out in little clouds wherever Tor looked. A few snowflakes spiraled lazily out of the gray sky.

Tor looked up at the mountains that had so amazed him when he had arrived with his mom yesterday. There was a huge flank of a mountain looming over the town. Hundreds of dots were swooping down the sides. Three enormous ski lifts swept up toward the top, and all Tor could see were the dangling skis and boards of the crazy people who were going to hop off the lifts and come screaming down the impossibly steep slopes of the mountain. In the distance were other mountains, covered with trees and lined with smooth white slopes and the thin wires and pylons of chairlifts. There was one mountain close to town that was an unbroken blanket of green trees. This mountain had no ski lifts, no broad avenues of snow, nothing. Tor wondered why this particular mountain was different.

"Excuse me," someone said, and Tor turned his gaze back to earth to see a pile of boxes and an annoyed-looking woman standing in front of him. She was holding the boxes.

"Sorry," he said, and stepped aside. The woman walked down the street, dressed from head to feet in a furry coat. The coat was shiny and very dark red, and it rippled as the woman moved. Tor realized it wasn't a fake. It was an actual mink coat. The only time he had ever seen such a thing was in old movies. People actually wore fur here?

Tor was getting colder standing still. He started walking again, looking for the Pro Shop. There was a selection of snowboards and boots in the window of the next shop on the street. That could be it.

Suddenly he was knocked, hard, in the shoulder. Tor staggered on the sidewalk, nearly falling down, and turned.

"Hey!" he said. The person who'd struck him was a teenager, in a blue coat that Tor recognized instantly. The snowboarding team member walked away. Tor couldn't see his face.

"Waster," the boy said clearly over his shoulder. It sounded like a taunt.

Tor thought of saying something, of trying to catch the kid and ask what he meant, but he had already disappeared up the street. Tor turned back, confused and angry, rubbing his shoulder. What was a "waster"? And why was he one?

"Hey," someone else said, and Tor turned around fast, thinking he was about to be hit again. Coach Rollins, now dressed in a police uniform, took a step back and put up his hands. He was standing with a tall man in a long camel-colored overcoat.

"Whoa now, settle down," Coach Rollins said. He smiled at Tor. "No muggers in this town, sport."

"Er, hi, sir," Tor said, shaking the hand Coach Rollins held out. Rollins didn't let go for a moment, squeezing hard, and then dropped Tor's hand. Tor resisted the urge to rub it and waited. He was more confused than ever.

"This is Mayor Malone, Tor. Mayor, this is Tor Sinclair, Dr. Sinclair's son."

"Pleased to meet you," the mayor said, putting out a

hand. Tor shook it gingerly, but the mayor's handshake was firm, not hard. He shook Tor's hand twice, a practiced double-pump, and let it go. His hands were covered in fine tan gloves. He smiled at Tor and it was such a warm, friendly smile that Tor should have felt better immediately. He didn't. The smile was so perfect, like the handshake, that he didn't trust it. The mayor's face was scrubbed and pink, and he had a big black mustache that reminded Tor of a Mr. Potato Head.

"So, what are you wandering about alone for on this fine day?" Rollins asked, smiling at Tor.

"Mom—my mom sent me to the Pro Shop, to get some snowboarding gear," Tor said, feeling uncomfortable. There were lots of kids on the street and not all of them had parents in tow. Was there a truant law or something?

"Ah, and here it is, right behind you," Rollins said, smiling all the while. "Enjoy your snowboarding lessons. We always enjoy making our visitors feel welcome here, don't we, sir?"

"Sure, sure we do," Mayor Malone said, smiling at Tor. "Nice to meet you, son."

"Thank you, sir," Tor said, and watched as the two men walked away. He didn't much like the mayor, although he couldn't exactly say why. And seeing Coach Rollins who was really Deputy Rollins was very strange.

Tor felt the oddest sensation, like the time he'd looked down through an open manhole on a busy street in San Diego. He'd seen tunnels, pipes, and thousands of wires of every color and width, and he got dizzy thinking that those things were under his feet *all the time*. Those pipes and lines and tunnels ran under every place he walked. This town was the same way, and that was a scary thought.

Tor blinked and realized he was still standing on the sidewalk. He opened the door of the Pro Shop, and a man came out of the back room as a bell that was attached to the door jingled cheerfully.

"Hello, how can I help you?" the man asked. He was tall and had a weathered tan. His hair was dark black but his eyes were a startling light brown, almost yellow.

"My mom sent me here," Tor said. "She wanted me to get suited up."

"For boarding? Or skiing?" the man asked kindly. "You're not a local? Wait . . . are you Dr. Sinclair's son?"

"That's right, I'm Tor," Tor said. "Torin Sinclair."

The man stood looking at Tor with a strange expression on his face. It couldn't be . . . pity? Then the expression was gone, and he smiled. "Nice to meet you, Tor," the man said, reaching out to shake his hand. His hand was large and warm and hard with calluses. "I'm Merrill Douglas. I'm so glad your mom decided to come give Snow Park a try. We need a doc so badly here, and we can't get one to stay."

"How come?" Tor asked.

"Look, I've got some things I have to do. How about

I take you back and let the kids outfit you, that way you can take your time. Get the best equipment. Follow me."

When Tor walked through the door Mr. Douglas held open, he found himself in a small room packed with skiing and boarding equipment. There was a workbench in the middle of the room and a machine that looked like a big grinder in one corner. A smell like burning candles filled the air.

A girl was holding a snowboard and rubbing the back of it with some sort of waxy stick. She looked up and smiled at Tor, and he smiled back. She was obviously Merrill Douglas's daughter, only instead of having light brown eyes, hers were as black as her long black braids. She was Tor's age, or close to it.

"Raine, meet Tor Sinclair," Mr. Douglas said. "I have to go. Suit him up, he's the new doc's kid. All paid for. Later."

"Later, Dad," Raine said.

"Raine?" Tor asked. "That's your name?"

"Raine, with an 'e.'" The voice wasn't Raine's—it came from a chair in a corner Tor hadn't seen, and there was a boy sitting in the chair. His hair was a caramel blond color. Tor had seen several of his kind in San Diego, actors' kids mostly, who had ended up with just the right combination of both parents' good looks. This kid would have fit right in with the Hollywood crowd, only he was wearing a big loose pair of brown pants and a sweater that was so incredibly ugly that Tor couldn't take his eyes off it. It looked like a blind grandma had taken every color from her basket and mixed them together and knitted something horrible. One sleeve was longer than the other, and there was a section of yarn that had pulled out into long tufts, like a patch of Bigfoot hair.

"That is the ugliest sweater I have ever seen," Tor said.

"It's warm," the boy said. He didn't smile. Tor swallowed. He'd only been trying to make a joke.

"Then I want one, too," Tor said finally. "This suit doesn't keep me warm at all."

"That suit is a piece of crap," the boy said. "Too tight for air flow, bad insulation. Cheap piece of crap."

"Okay," Tor said. "I don't think my mom knows how to pick out cold weather stuff."

"That's why she sent you here," Raine said. She finished waxing the snowboard and set it carefully on a stand, then wiped her hands on a cloth. Her hands were small and square. Her braids hung halfway down her back and were so glossy they had blue highlights in the light.

"You're the doctor's son," the boy said.

"Yeah, I guess so," Tor said. "Is that a good thing or a bad thing?"

"A bad thing, probably," the boy said.

"Oh, shut up, Drake," Raine said. She reached out to shake Tor's hand. Her grip was strong and her hands were callused, like her father's. "We'll get you warmed up. Your mom told my dad to set you up with the best. Snowboard pants, coat, thermal underwear, gloves, hat, and a sweater that doesn't look like a dog threw up on it. This is Drake Wexler, by the way."

"Tor," Tor said.

"Tor is short for?" asked Drake.

"Torin," Tor said. "But I prefer Tor."

"Tor then," Raine said. "I hear you're from California."

"It's warm there," Tor said.

"Beaches?" Drake said, half-standing so he could shake Tor's hand, too. It seemed oddly formal, kids shaking hands like grown-ups, but Tor liked it.

"Sand, too," Tor said. "I miss it. But I'm supposed to learn snowboarding, so maybe I won't miss surfing so much."

This wasn't precisely true. Tor's family had lived more than two hours inland from the beach, and they hadn't been able to make the trip to the ocean once since Tor's stepmom had gotten pregnant with the twins. Not that he was about to tell anyone that, of course. Everyone who wasn't from California seemed to think everyone in California lived on a beach and went surfing every day.

Drake sank back into his chair, which Tor saw was an ancient overstuffed leather club chair that looked like Sherlock Holmes had just gotten out of it to go light his pipe.

"Excellent!" Raine said happily. "Pay no attention to Drake. You're going to love snowboarding if you like surfing." Raine flipped up a laptop that Tor hadn't seen amid all the equipment on her desk. She typed quickly. "I've got Gloria free at one o'clock. She'll take you until four."

"Three hours?" Tor asked, disappointed. He was hoping for more. Drake and Raine looked at each other and smirked.

"You're going to feel like you've been drop-kicked out of a speeding car by this time tomorrow," Drake said.

"Three hours your first time is enough," Raine said, still typing. She hit a final key with a flourish and shut the laptop. "She'll arrange your schedule after your first day, so ask her about your next lessons. Now let's get you geared up."

"Why bother?" Drake asked.

"Because this isn't the only place to snowboard in the universe, Mr. Know-It-All," Raine said sharply. "Even if they don't stay, we can try to teach him to board."

"Why wouldn't I stay?" asked Tor. "Hey, and by the way, what's a 'waster'?"

"A waste of oxygen," Raine said. "Worse than a loser. Drake, get your butt out of the chair and help me, or I'm not helping you with your English essay."

"Essay? Aren't you on break?" Tor asked, suddenly feeling panicked.

"This is the last day of break," Drake said, heaving

himself out of the chair. Tor realized the table sitting next to Drake was full of textbooks, not snow equipment. "I've got a late essay I'm turning in on Monday. I'm just blocked on essays. I can't get it at all. Raine here, she's a whiz at writing. But she can't figure out an algebra equation to save her life. So we tutor each other."

"How's the school?" Tor asked. "Hopeless? Okay?"

"It's hopeless. Of course. It's school. One word of warning," Drake said, rummaging through a box in the corner of the shop. "This is a small town. The teachers already know everything about you."

"The teachers know everything? How do the teachers know everything?" Tor asked.

"Because the town knows everything," Raine said.

"Not *everything*," Drake said. Raine threw up her hands and shrugged, and started to rummage in a bin full of snowboards.

"Let's see, you're going to grow this year but you're a newbie, so we'll put you in a one-forty-nine-centimeter board," she murmured.

"Thermals," Drake said, throwing a packet at Tor. He caught them and examined the cover. A man who looked like a ballet dancer was wearing tights and a long-sleeved shirt. He looked like a complete tool.

"That's just the underwear," Drake said, and grinned a bit. "Go in there and get those on, and I'll throw you in some boarding pants."

"This isn't some new-kid hazing thing, is it?" Tor asked suspiciously. "Because I don't think hazing is very funny."

"Don't worry, we're both wearing thermals," said Raine, smiling. "Look." She peeled up a corner of her shirt and Tor could see the top of long underwear pants and a shirt of the same thin material. "Drake?"

"Oh, I suppose," Drake said, and lifted his hideous sweater. "Now get those on so you can stop shivering. You're practically blue."

"Mottled purple, I'd say," Raine said cheerfully.

Within a half hour Tor was feeling better than he had since he'd stepped out of his mom's warm car yesterday into the cold Colorado mountains. The thermals were tight but they immediately stopped all the tiny drafts that made his skin goosebump all over, and the snowboarder's pants were not just roomy and comfortable, they were warm as well. The knees were padded, and there seemed to be an unending supply of zippers and pockets.

"Just like the town," Drake said, when Tor marveled at an internal pocket that had a zipper outside and two zippered pockets on the inside. "Lots of secrets."

"Do I get a sweater?" Tor asked, ignoring Drake. He wasn't an idiot. There was a secret he should know, but they weren't going to tell him. Fine. He wasn't going to beg. "Can I get one just like yours?"

"You're not good-looking enough," Drake said loftily.

"He means, that's his signature—awful sweaters. He's got a closet full of them. It's the whole looks thing," Raine said with an irritated sigh. If Drake was irresistible to most girls, Raine obviously wasn't one of them.

"Oh," Tor said. "I guess so. In San Diego you'd be one in about a hundred actors' kids, I think. Ugly sweaters wouldn't do, you'd sweat to death."

Raine burst into laughter and punched Drake in the arm. He pretended to stagger, fell back into his Sherlock chair, and smiled at Tor for the first time.

"Well, that answers why you weren't all strange around me, like all the other guys," Drake said.

Tor was struggling to get into a soft jersey that Raine had handed him. "Other guys are strange?" Tor asked.

"I look different," Drake said gloomily, slouching further into his chair. "Plus, my dad is Todd Wexler. So that's another load I have to carry."

"Why?" Tor asked.

"He's Todd Wexler," Drake said, then snorted at Tor's look of puzzlement. "Whoa, I forgot. You're not a snowboarder."

"He's a world-famous snowboarder," Raine explained, not looking the least impressed. "But he's not exactly the greatest dad. Plus, all the women in this town—including everybody's mom—have a thing for him."

"Raine," Drake said, and Raine snapped her mouth shut like a trap.

"You don't act all funny around him," Tor pointed out, getting an arm through the jersey sleeve.

"I'm just who I am," Raine said. "Drake and I, we've been friends since kindergarten. Now it looks like there's somebody else in town who doesn't think much of your looks either, Drake."

"They're nice looks, I guess," Tor said, finally tugging his jersey into position. "It's just, I went to school for a while with Serena Davis's kids. You know, the Oscar winner last year? I mean, honestly."

"Dropped off by limo every day?" Raine asked, her black eyes alight.

"Hummers, two of them. One for the security detail," Tor said.

"Cool!" Raine said.

"Kicking," Drake admitted.

"They'd hang with you," Tor said comfortingly, and Drake started laughing.

Raine's dad, Mr. Douglas, shouldered his way into the room carrying a huge snowboard. It was still wet and dripped snow onto the floor.

"Raine, can you wax this . . ." He trailed off, looking at Drake. Drake stopped laughing instantly and the smile disappeared from his face. He got up from the chair and started rummaging around in some square boxes that held what looked like bear traps, as though he was embarrassed at being caught laughing like that. Tor had no idea why.

"Funny joke," he muttered as Mr. Douglas set the board on Raine's waxing platform. "I'm getting you some bindings, Tor."

"Must have been a good joke," Mr. Douglas said, looking from Drake to Tor and then to Raine. "Got a lesson set up for him, Raine?"

"Got it, Dad," Raine said. "Gloria at one o'clock. Wax job?"

"And tighten the bindings." Mr. Douglas left the room with a sad expression on his face.

"What is it about me?" Tor asked nobody in particular.

"He feels guilty," Drake said quietly, and handed a stick of something to Raine. She lit a small device and the smell of wax filled the air.

"Why?" Tor asked in frustration, even though he'd promised himself he wouldn't. "Why would he feel guilty about me?"

Raine turned on the wheel that spread hot wax over the snowboard, and the shrill sound of the motor filled the room. Drake held up some of the bear trap–looking things—the bindings—and gestured at the snowboard Raine had leaned against the wall.

No one could talk as Raine carefully moved the big snowboard back and forth across the wheel. A loud grinding noise and a smell like burnt candles filled the room, but suddenly Tor didn't notice. Tor had forgotten everything except what now leaned against the wall.

The snowboard was glossy smooth, and the design on the front was a beach sunset with nothing but the yellow ball of the sun dipping below orange waves. A single pointed black triangle of a shark's fin cut the water.

The board was the most beautiful thing Tor had ever seen. He looked back at Raine, and she glanced up and winked at him, then returned to her noisy waxing task. *Yes,* her wink said. *This is your board.* Tor ran a smooth hand down the board and felt something he couldn't quite name rise up inside him.

He was going to stay here. He was going to learn how to make that snowboard surf the mountain. And no one was going to drive him away.

He turned to see Drake looking at him with sad eyes. Drake said something that Tor couldn't catch over the whine of the waxing motor. Tor took the board and pointed at the bindings Drake held in his hands. He pointed at his new board, eyebrows raised.

Drake shrugged, and gave Tor a nod. *So be it,* his nod seemed to say. *Your funeral.*

3 ✠ RINGING THE BELL

GLORIA MIGHT HAVE had a last name, but she didn't need one if she did. Tor stood with his new board, in his new boots, with his helmet under his arm, staring at his snowboard instructor.

"You must be Tor," Gloria said, and her perfect mouth parted in a smile of dazzling white. "I'm Gloria." She was apple-cheeked and blue-eyed and wore her long hair in two blond braids. Her red jacket had a Snow Park crest on the front pocket, and one gloved hand rested on a tall snowboard that was propped in the snow next to her. The snowboard was as yellow as her hair and had big white daisies printed on it. She was at least six feet tall, maybe more. Tall, anyway.

"I'm Tor," he said, and remembered to close his mouth. He was at the entrance to the Snow Park Lodge, a big wooden building at the base of Snow Mountain.

The sky was overcast and a few snowflakes fell. There were lots of people in outfits of every color swooping down the slopes, some on skis and some on boards. There were lines of people getting on the chairlifts, all of them puffing cheerful clouds of breath around their heads. Some were coated with powdery snow. One group of children in a single-file line glided toward the chairlifts, led like a mother duck by a tall boy dressed in a red jacket just like Gloria's.

"That's the boarding class," Gloria said, following Tor's gaze. "Don't worry, you don't need to be a little kid to learn to ride. You'll be on your feet in no time."

"Okay," Tor said, gripping his board with his mittens. "Where do I start?"

"With your lift pass," Gloria said, and nodded at the building behind them. "You get a free lift pass because your mom's the doc, so let's go get your tag and we'll get started."

Tor followed her into the depths of the lodge. Cries of "Gloria!" and "Yo, Gloria!" followed them as they worked their way back to the season-pass office. Tor realized for once no one was looking at him: everyone was looking at Gloria. Tor rather liked it. He was already tired of the sidelong glances, the looks, and the remarks that he didn't understand.

He looked into the digital camera that a lodge employee held up—the man chatting with Gloria all the while so that Tor wondered if the picture would even have his head in it—and then he was presented with a warm plastic badge on a lanyard. His head was right in the center of the picture, more by luck than anything else, he thought.

"Now the fun part," Gloria said, rubbing her hands together. "We're going to go to the bunny slope first, and I'll show you how to put on your gear. Are you regular or goofy?"

Tor was ready for this one. "Regular" meant you had your left foot forward on the board. "Goofy" meant your right foot was forward.

"I'm goofy," he said, and bit back a very childish laugh. His dad was the only person on the planet who knew that Tor's favorite cartoon character was Goofy. Tor thought Goofy was the greatest. Tor's runner-up favorite was Wile E. Coyote, which made his father suggest mournfully that Tor look for a future in test engineering. This memory gave Tor such a wave of homesickness that he had to grip his hands tight in his big snowboarder mittens for a minute and try to think of something else.

The test to determine that he was goofy was simple and kind of funny. Sort of Wile E. Coyote, actually. Before Drake had put on Tor's snowboard bindings in the warm room at the back of the Pro Shop, Drake stood up from his chair. Without warning, Drake shoved Tor in the chest. Tor took a quick step back with his left foot, and both Drake and Raine had shouted, "You're goofy!"

They explained that when a person is suddenly unbalanced, they step back with one foot. That foot is the dominant, or back foot, on the board. Simple.

"Great!" Gloria said. "I'm goofy, too. That'll make things easier. Let's trudge on over to the beginner's slope and we'll get started."

Boarders and skiers whizzed by as they walked over to Powder Hill. Tor realized this was where the Flight for Life helicopter had landed the night before. It looked almost completely flat in the bright daylight, and he was disappointed. He looked upslope and saw a snowboarder cruising down, the end of his board flicking casually back and forth like the tail of a big cat, his body loose and relaxed.

"That's what you're going to be like," Gloria said, following Tor's gaze. "See how he's standing on the board? He's not crouched, he's not completely upright, he's just in-between."

They reached a spot that looked like every other spot on the broad white slope. Gloria flipped her board over and set it, bindings down, into the snow.

"Rule one," she said, turning to him. "Always set your board down with the bindings face down in the snow unless you're in them, or you'll be chasing your board down the hill. Rule two: wear a leash at all times. That's the strap that holds your board to your boot. If you're not wearing a leash and your board comes off while you're on the chairlift, your board will fall and could kill someone. Wear a leash. And rule three: wear a helmet. Your mom can tell you all about head injuries. I help out with the Ski Patrol sometimes, so I know, too. Wear your helmet."

"Okay," Tor said.

"Let's gear you up," Gloria said, her eyes sparkling. "You've got a sweet little setup there. Nice board, the best bindings, good helmet. Sweet!"

Gloria made Tor get in and out of his bindings twice, and she adjusted the bindings with a sturdy screwdriver from her pocket before she was satisfied. As she was working on his board, a couple of boys skied by, staring at her, and the taller one ran right into the shorter one. They both fell in a tangle of legs and arms and skis. They picked themselves up sheepishly and poled away. Tor bit his lip to keep from laughing.

Finally Gloria nodded, and showed Tor how to sit in the snow, the classic snowboarder's stance. Bottom in the snow, board crosswise to the mountain, knees up.

"Now watch me," Gloria said, and strapped in. She stood up and relaxed into the same catlike stance as the rider they'd watched come down the mountain. She snapped the chin strap on her helmet and settled her goggles over her eyes. Tor waited to see her plunge away in some amazing trick, but instead she pointed her hand in front of her, slid very gently about ten feet, and slid to a stop by moving the back of the board out to the side.

"That's it?" Tor said.

"That's it," Gloria said, from ten feet away. "It won't feel right at first. Just point, slide, and see what happens."

Tor stood up, and the board immediately started sliding away with him. He tried to relax, tried to point, and forgot completely about anything but trying to keep on his feet. The board was suddenly in the air and Tor's head slammed into the snow.

"Hey, that was great!" Gloria said, her face appearing in the sky above Tor's head. "You actually got on your feet the first time. Nice."

"That was nice?" Tor said, his head ringing.

"It takes a lot of practice," Gloria said. "You'll get it. On your feet, soldier!"

By four o'clock Tor felt, as Drake had predicted, like he'd been drop-kicked out of a speeding car. Every part of his body was sore. None of the old rules applied when he felt his body start to fall. He couldn't move his feet because they were strapped into a board. His arms would flail around wildly, his head would swing like a bob at the end of a pendulum, and his face or his backside would slam into the snow.

"You really rang the bell today, eh?" Gloria asked, helping him unstrap from his bindings. He'd managed a glide of about ten feet before falling, and Gloria applauded like he'd won the Olympics. Then he fell, and she called it a day.

"I fell a lot, yeah," Tor said.

"No worries. You're going to be an awesome rider," Gloria said. "Really, you are."

"Yeah?" Tor said, and couldn't help grinning at her. She really was nice under all that pretty.

"Yeah," she said. "You've got great balance, you've got great reflexes, all you need to do is keep working at it. You coming back tomorrow, then?"

"Uh, I think I have school," Tor said, forgetting his aches and wondering if he could somehow get out of classes tomorrow. The day after that, too. Forever, if possible.

"How about three-thirty, right after school. See you then?"

"Yes," Tor said firmly. Gloria gave him a mock salute and then she slid away.

He trudged slowly back to the lodge, his heavy snowboard under his arm, suddenly realizing he was more hungry than he'd ever been in his life. His entire middle felt hollowed out. He didn't have any pocket money, or he would have bought a burger at the lodge cafeteria. As it was, the smell of the burgers and the French fries nearly drove him mad. He clumped through the lodge and walked up the main street of Snow Park, the board getting heavier and heavier in his arms. When he reached his mom's clinic, he saw in the reflection of the glass in the window that he was still wearing his helmet, so he took it off.

"Mom?" he called, walking inside. He stopped. A lady dressed in white sat at the desk where the snowboarding team had crowded around Brian Slader the night before.

"You must be Tor, right?" the woman said. "I'm Mrs. Colm, her assistant. I'm afraid Dr. Sinclair is with a patient right now. I don't want to disturb her." Mrs. Colm was elderly and thin, with straight gray hair that was tucked behind her ears and curved smoothly around her head. She smiled at Tor, but it wasn't a very friendly smile. She looked a lot like the seagulls that snatched food at the beach. She had the same bright eye and sharp look.

"I just thought I could—" Tor started. He was going to say "rummage through her purse and get money out," but he stopped. He would do that to his dad's wallet, and as long as he let his dad know he'd taken money from the "petty cash account," as his dad said, the arrangement worked out well.

But Tor had no idea if that was the way his mom worked. The receptionist looked at him with unreadable clear gray eyes, eyes that looked like all the other people in Snow Park who whispered and pointed. Tor had completely forgotten about that while he was taking a lesson in snowboarding. Now he felt all that weight come back on his shoulders, and he turned without another word and clumped out of the clinic.

At home, after three peanut butter and jelly sandwiches and two big glasses of milk, Tor started to feel better. He put the plate and glass in the dishwasher and searched in the kitchen until he found a soft cloth. He wiped down his snowboard the way Raine had taught him, keeping it dry and clean so the metal edges wouldn't rust.

Tor's mom walked in while he was still rubbing his board dry. He looked up. Dr. Sinclair was dressed in a green parka with fur around the collar, but she looked cold and tired. Her nose was red.

"Tor," she said. "Hi. How were lessons?"

"Great," he said. "I came by—didn't Mrs. Colm tell you?"

His mother froze and her lips tightened. "She didn't tell me!"

"She said you were with a patient," Tor said calmly, checking the back of his board for scrapes. He ran his hands up and down the glossy board, checking for moisture, avoiding his mother's gaze.

"I would have come out for a minute, at least," Dr. Sinclair said. "It was only a sprained wrist. I'll have to speak to her."

Suddenly Dr. Sinclair sat down at the table, still in

her parka. She put a hand to her forehead like she had a headache.

"Mom?" he asked. "You okay?"

"I'm okay," she said. "Mrs. Colm is married to one of the clinic directors. That's all. I have to tread carefully here. I can't go shouting at her, even if I want to."

"But you're a doctor," Tor said in surprise.

"Doctors aren't like little gods," Dr. Sinclair said with a rueful smile at Tor. "We can get hired and fired just like everybody else. This town hired me, and I have to be careful to keep the boat from rocking."

Tor said something to his board, and his mother frowned. "What?" she said.

"I thought all that ended after you got out of school," Tor said grimly, and his mother surprised him by giving a great shout of laughter.

"Oh, how I wish it did," she said. "I'll talk to Mrs. Colm and tell her you're always allowed to wait in my office. And I'll give you my beeper number so you can page me. That way, she won't be offended and you won't have to go hungry."

"I'm not hungry," Tor said. "I ate already."

"Oh, you did?" Dr. Sinclair said, disappointed. "What did you have?"

"PB&J," Tor said.

"Well, make me a couple of them, would you?" Dr. Sinclair said. She stood up and shrugged out of her coat. "I'm going to change out of these scrubs and into some warmer clothes, and then maybe we can go over your schedule for school."

"Milk?" Tor asked. He was oddly pleased to be making his mom dinner, even if it was just peanut butter and jelly.

"Big glass," his mom yelled from down the hall, and Tor grinned to himself as he opened the fridge.

Tor tried to hold on to that cozy feeling the next day, his first day of school. The other thing he held on to was the thought of his board, sitting in his room at home and waiting for him.

Everyone knew each other—that was the first hard part. He wasn't a new kid in a sea of new kids, like it had been every year of school in Los Angeles and then San Diego. Here he was entering school in the middle of the school year. He was the *only* new kid, the doctor's kid, and something about being the doctor's kid held a secret that no one wanted to explain.

Snow Park Middle/High School was a combined school because the district was so small that kids from sixth through twelfth grades attended. The school was older than his past couple of schools in California, where the buildings were all big glass cubes. Tor liked this graceful old brick building. The school had tall, narrow windows and heavy double doors that looked like they were made of brass. It looked like a castle, with tall towers on each end of the building and stone arches along the roofline. He looked for gargoyles. There should be gargoyles somewhere. He didn't spot any.

Tor's first class was English, and he found the room without a problem. Drake and Raine were there, and he felt a burst of relief when he saw them. Here were two people he knew.

The classroom was old but well cared for. The oak around the windows gleamed with warm yellow. Actual radiators lined the wall near the window, and a black chalkboard ran the width of the room where a teacher stood, papers in hand, staring at him as though she had been turned to stone.

"Ms. Petrus?" Tor asked.

"You must be Torin Sinclair," Ms. Petrus said with a start, coming alive. "Welcome to our class." She didn't sound very welcoming, though.

Ms. Petrus was tall and had black hair pulled back in a clasp. She had eyes as dark as her hair and the hugest nose Tor had ever seen. She wasn't ugly, though. She looked almost queenly, like carvings Tor had seen in pictures of Egyptian tombs, right down to the imperious lift of her chin. If she'd been wearing a Cleopatra costume, she'd have been a dead ringer.

"Thanks," Tor said, trying on a polite smile, and started to head toward Drake and Raine.

"We have assigned seating in our classes," Ms. Petrus said coldly. "You'll be sitting here."

"Here" meant at the front corner of the room, right

in front of Ms. Petrus. Tor sighed and took a seat. The teacher set down a stack of papers and another stack of books.

"Here are your books and this week's schoolwork," Ms. Petrus said. "I don't know about your previous school district, so we'll just have to assess how things are going after the first week. Okay?"

"Yes, ma'am," Tor said.

That was the way it went all day. *Yes, ma'am* and *yes, sir,* and more and more schoolbooks until Tor's backpack was so heavy he could barely lift it. When he was heading for the lunchroom, Tor was elbowed into the wall so hard he felt his teeth clack together and the door next to him rattled as the old smoked glass vibrated in the frame.

"Waster," someone sneered, but Tor didn't see who it was. He hunched his shoulders and gripped his backpack and thought about his snowboard.

When Tor walked into the school lunchroom, he eyed it with suspicion. Lunch was always the worst at any new school. He got a tray and resigned himself to finding some place all by himself. He kept a firm grip on his tray and watched closely for feet stuck out to trip him. His family had moved a lot before his mom had left to go to medical school—his dad was in real estate investing, and that meant a lot of moves. After his mom had left and his parents had divorced, Tor and his dad had moved even more. Tor had been in at least three elementary schools and two middle schools before Snow Park.

Then he saw Raine and Drake sitting alone. Tor cautiously raised an eyebrow at them. Raine nodded once. He walked toward them and a slight whisper ran over the lunchroom through the loud clatter and noise. Tor saw heads turn toward him as he took a seat by Raine.

"Thanks," he said briefly.

"Raine likes to upset the social order whenever possible," Drake said with a sharp, almost angry smile. "We're supposed to hate you, of course. So we ask you to sit with us. This is so confusing some people's heads might actually explode. How was glorious Gloria?"

"Terrific. I'm going to have another lesson after school," Tor said. "I'm sore all over."

"She's great, though, isn't she?" Raine said.

"Yeah," Tor said happily, and Raine nodded in satisfaction. Drake flipped open an algebra book and for the next half hour, Tor ate while Drake taught Raine about the quadratic equation. It was the most peaceful time he'd had all day.

The last class of the day was choir, a choice that Tor had initially protested the night before when his mom went over his schedule.

"Choir? You've got to be kidding," he had said, looking at his mother with outrage and embarrassment. "You signed me up for *choir*?"

"Music is mandatory here," his mom had said, shrugging. "You have to choose orchestra, band, or choir. Honestly. I know you don't play an instrument, so I had to put you in choir."

Tor entered the choir room late because he had trouble finding his way to the auditorium. There was a big crowd of kids packed into circular risers, all of them chattering like seagulls at the beach. The noise died away as Tor entered the room. He felt his face heat up as all those eyes turned toward him, and he felt the weight of their interest.

"Tor," a woman said, coming forward to shake his hand. "I'm Ms. Adams. Nice to meet you." Tor realized that this teacher, unlike all the other ones, actually meant it.

Ms. Adams was very short and very slender. She had fair, freckled skin and vivid red hair that curled wildly around her face. She was dressed in soft dark brown pants and a green velvet sweater, and her pointed face looked a lot like an elf's. Tor couldn't see her ears and wondered if they were pointed, too.

"Do you know your range?" Ms. Adams asked.

"Range?" Tor replied, confused.

"Are you a bass, a tenor, or a baritone?" she asked. "Never mind. Take a seat with the baritones and we'll see."

Tor found a seat and didn't have to scrunch down because the two boys on either side made room for him.

They made a lot of room, with expressions on their faces like they smelled something bad. Tor stifled a sigh and took his seat.

"Let's get some work done," Ms. Adams said, and everyone whipped out sheet music from their packs. Ms. Adams passed a sheet up to Tor and he looked at it blankly. He'd never seen sheet music up close before.

"This is called 'Angels We Have Heard on High,' " Ms. Adams said crisply. "We'll be performing this at our holiday concert, so let's get everything just perfect."

At the end of the hour, when the three o'clock bell rang, Tor had forgotten all about watching the clock. He'd never taken any voice lessons before and he had no idea how a choir sang songs. Ms. Adams had worked the soprano section through a difficult piece while everyone else sat and listened intently. Tor saw Raine with that group. Then Ms. Adams worked the bass section of boys, where Drake sat, then the alto girls, and finally the baritones. Each section sang the same words but in a different range. Tor mouthed the words. He really had no idea how to sing.

Then Ms. Adams raised her stick, everyone rose to their feet, the student at the piano started to play, and all the pieces came together. Tor could hear every range of voice all blended into one, and it sounded completely different than before. The sound was amazing, because he was right in the center of it all, hearing the "o" sound, up and down like a snowboard going over bumps. The "o" was the "o" sound in Gloria, in a language Ms. Adams had told them was Latin: "Gloria in excelsis deo." The song was nearly as pretty as his snowboarding teacher.

Before he thought about the time, the bell rang and the class gathered their bags and thundered out of the room, talking and laughing. Tor gathered his things more slowly, hoping the corridor would be empty when he left class. This choir class had been a good way to end his day and he didn't want to walk home remembering being slammed into a locker.

"You'll be a baritone, I think," Ms. Adams said to Tor, startling him so that he nearly dropped his sheet music.

"Uh, thanks," he said, not knowing what else to say. He actually hadn't sung a single note.

"I'm new here, too," Ms. Adams said suddenly, and Tor looked up to see her at the front of the room, arms folded, still carrying her little stick in the crook of her arm. She really did look like an elf. Her directing stick even looked like a wand. Did elves carry wands? Tor wasn't sure.

"Oh," he said, zipping his bag closed.

"I've only been here two years, which is like yesterday to this town. You want to talk to someone, I'm always here," said Ms. Adams. "An outside opinion, as it were. Just remember. I'm here."

This gave Tor a little bit of comfort as he walked out of the choir room. He was happy to see that the hallways were empty as he headed for his locker. As he came to a corner, he heard voices and stopped instantly, as wary as a deer.

"You really think the curse made Brian sick?" The person sounded fearful.

"Of course it did," another voice said angrily. "He's a great rider and he's in great shape. There was nothing wrong with him!"

"But you know, what he has us do, don't you think that might—"

"No way. He told us we'd be okay, and we are, aren't we? We're winning races all the time!"

"Yeah, but Brian—"

"That's the curse. The rest of us, we're all fine, aren't we? The curse, that's what made him sick. You know we have to get that doctor out of town, or somebody else is gonna get sick. Maybe die."

"Yeah," the timid first person said, sounding stronger and more sure. "You're right."

"Let's go. I'm sick of this place," the other voice said, and Tor got ready to run if they headed his direction.

Their footsteps went the other way and Tor was alone, his heart pounding, wondering what the snowboarders were talking about. What were they doing? And who was the *he* that was making them do it? Tor opened his locker and shouldered his book bag and headed home, the questions in his head spinning uselessly like a hamster in a wheel.

He was almost home when he glanced up. The resort slopes were full of skiers and snowboarders. They looked like black dots on a field of white. He had forgotten he had a snowboarding lesson! He broke into a clumsy run, his book bag thumping against his back.

The schoolbooks went on his bed, and Tor was in his boarding clothes and out the door. His snowboard rested in his elbow, and he felt everything fall away as he headed for Snow Park Lodge and the mountain beyond.

4 ☠ COMPLICATIONS

"YOU'RE UP, YOU'RE up!" shouted Gloria, and that was when Tor caught an edge with his snowboard and smashed into the snow with his face. He skidded downhill and lifted his head up to gasp after he spit icy cold snow from his mouth. Snow packed his goggles. He lifted his snowboard with his feet and flipped so he faced downhill and sat up, still gasping.

A sound like someone tearing a piece of paper in two announced the arrival of Gloria. She sat down in the snow next to him.

"I'm okay," he said, and started laughing. She grinned and gave him a whack on the back.

"Let's rest for a minute," she said, and put her elbows on her knees.

The town spread below them like a toy village. The day had cleared and the sun was a brilliant electric blue, as blue as Gloria's eyes. Without goggles the snow would have been too dazzling to look at. Tor wiped out his goggles and got the last of the snow off his face.

The chairlift line was busy, constantly hauling riders and skiers up the mountain. Two snowboarders whooshed by, one of them shouting "Yo, Gloria!"

"Hey!" she called back. "Isn't this the life, Tor?"

"Sure is," he said. The sky stretched above him. The deep green of the trees poked through their frosting of white powder. He could still feel the sensation of being up and riding a snowboard. It was exactly like the dreams he'd had as a small child, of flying through the sky without wings or plane, being able to swoop and soar however he liked.

"Time for the chairlift," Gloria said, and hopped to her feet. "You're ready for a real slope."

Tor knew what he was supposed to do, but he found himself a little scared as he and Gloria reached the head of the line and moved out to the loading line. The chairlift, so slow from a distance, now seemed to be rushing toward him. He reached for the bar and the chair scooped him up and then he was trying not to pant as he and Gloria were lifted into the air. She grinned at him and gave him a satisfied nod.

Giant concrete pylons marched up the slope ahead of them. Their chair bumped over the first pylon's supporting arm. Gloria looked at the slopes, watching other snowboarders and skiers, and then she saw something that caught her attention.

"Look, Tor," she said, pointing at the next pylon. There was a man in a Ski Patrol outfit and he was buried up to his head in the snow right next to the pylon. Tor blinked in surprise. That couldn't be right. Then the man moved and Tor saw that he was standing in a hole in the snow.

"The pylons have an access hatch on the downslope slide," Gloria explained as they swept up to the pylon. "There's wiring and mechanical checks that have to be made every week on these big boys." The man climbed out of a hatch that was surrounded by thick orange padding. The padding went all the way around the concrete pylon.

"Smashing into a tree isn't much better, but the pylons are always padded to prevent accidents," Gloria explained. They bumped over the pylon's supporting arm and Gloria shook her snowboard, hard. The chair rocked and Tor gasped. Snow fell from Gloria's board and thumped on the head of the Ski Patrolman below. He was just closing the hatch, and Tor caught a glimpse of a ladder leading down into darkness.

"Hey!" the man said angrily, and then he saw Gloria and his expression melted into the same sappy smile that everybody wore around her. "Hey, Gloria!"

"Hey, Rob," Gloria called out, and then they were

past and heading toward the next pylon and the top of the mountain.

Gloria had coached Tor patiently on getting off a chairlift with a snowboard attached to one leg, but he fell anyway. Gloria, neatly hopping out of his way, came back to help him to his feet.

"Ready?" Gloria asked, and Tor nodded. "Okay then, let's do the falling leaf again. Turn your board against the hill to go sideways, go straight for a bit, then back against the hill. Falling gently like a leaf." She demonstrated by hopping to her feet and sliding gently down the hill. "Aim straight forward," she said, and pointed the tip of her board down the hill. "Heel side!" She brought her snowboard around with her heels and she stopped going forward and instead slid across the slope.

"Heel side, go straight, heel side," Tor murmured, and got to his feet.

He started to slide across the hill, and he crouched down a bit and tried to relax into the cat crouch of a snowboarder. Then he pointed the tip of his board down the hill and instantly he was going fast, straight down. He kicked his back heel forward and just like that, he was slowing down and gently sliding across the slope.

Gloria, watching him, gave a big yip of delight and pumped her arm in the air. Tor ignored her and tried the same move again. Straight forward, go very fast. Kick the heel around, slow down.

"I think I got it," he said to himself, trying it again. "I think I got it!"

"Woooo!" Gloria shouted. A snowboarder dressed in neon plaid pants so loud they seemed to leave a plaid image in the air behind him shot by, laughing, and returned Gloria's yell. "Keep going!" Gloria shouted to Tor.

Tor made his way down the rest of the hill without falling. He stopped close to the chairlifts and stood, trembling a little but not enough that anyone could see. Gloria shot down the slope and came to a stop by turning her board and blasting Tor with a long white arc of snow that covered him from head to foot.

"Hey!"

"It's tradition," Gloria laughed. "You made it down the hill! I'm supposed to rub your face in the snow, but I never liked doing that."

"Thanks," Tor said, wiping at his coat and pants, grinning like crazy.

"We're done for today," Gloria said. "Tomorrow, you come here by yourself and practice falling leaf. Then we'll teach you on Wednesday how to do an S-curve."

"What's that?"

"The back-and-forth move. You've got one part of it," Gloria said, reaching down and unbuckling one of her boots from her board. She stood upright and gave him one of her dazzling smiles. "You don't need me whooping and hollering at you. You take a day by yourself to learn this part. We'll have you doing the half-pipe in no time."

Tor felt himself get prickles with the thought of doing half-pipe tricks. He suddenly lost his balance and sat down in the snow. Gloria giggled and leaned over to scoop up some snow. She pushed off and her snowboard glided away toward the chairlifts.

"See you day after, Tor," she called, and pegged him perfectly in the center of his chest with a snowball.

Tor released his bindings and took off his helmet and walked off the slope and through the lodge in a happy sort of dream state, imagining himself flying down the half-pipe and flipping in midair, making everyone gasp and then applaud and applaud for Tor Sinclair, champion snowboarder.

He abruptly came to earth when he reached home and found his mom sitting at the kitchen table, her head in her hands. The daylight was quickly turning to deep winter night, but the lights were off.

"Mom, are you okay?" Tor asked from the doorway. He'd turned on the light in the utility room so he could get out of his wet snowboarding clothes and nearly jumped out of his skin when he saw his mother sitting silently in the gloom of the kitchen.

"Hi, Tor," his mom said, not looking at him. She looked very tired.

"Are you okay?"

"I lost a patient," she said. "My first patient, actually. Brian Slader, you saw him. He died at Denver General this afternoon."

Tor forgot about his wet things and sat down at the table. He took his mom's hand in his. It was icy cold.

"I'm sorry, Mom," he said awkwardly. He remembered how his mom had said Brian Slader was going to be okay. "How did he die?"

This was evidently the right thing to say. Dr. Sinclair looked suddenly angry. "Exactly!" she said. "He shouldn't have died. He was manifesting a rather mild case of pulmonary edema. No one knows why some people get that at high altitudes, but the prognosis is always good if you can get them down in altitude. But Slader's red blood cell count was terribly low. I've looked over the charts. They kept putting units of blood in him and they still couldn't get his system over the initial shock of all that blood loss."

"It didn't seem like that much blood," Tor said, thinking of the bloody pink foam at Brian Slader's mouth.

"It wasn't. There's no reason for that much loss. Maybe he was bleeding internally. The autopsy will tell us. Tor, you're soaking wet! Get out of those clothes right now."

Tor got up from the table. His mom stood up and turned on a light and started fussing in the refrigerator.

She wasn't sitting still in the dark kitchen anymore, and that was good.

They ate paella, a dish of rice and spices with lots of chunks of different kinds of meat and seafood. Tor had visited his mom in Detroit last summer and she'd taken him to a restaurant that served paella.

"I remembered how you liked it, so I figured out how to make it for you," his mom said in an offhand way, scooping a big bowl for Tor and another, smaller one for herself. She smiled at him and ruffled his hair. He rolled his eyes at her and she laughed.

Later, after two bowls of hot paella and two glasses of cold milk, Tor sat at the table while his mom washed up. He started looking through his homework. He found himself telling his mom about the Egyptian queen English teacher, Ms. Petrus, and the math teacher, Mr. Ewald, who was as round as an egg and bald too, who looked just like Humpty Dumpty. He even wore a bow tie.

"Justin Ewald," Dr. Sinclair laughed, drying the glasses they'd used. "What a perfect description!"

"He seems okay," Tor said. His mom took a seat at the table and pulled his English papers toward her.

"Who else?" she asked, looking at the papers.

"Ms. Adams, the choir teacher. I think I'm going to like choir. It's a lot more fun than I thought."

"Kaia Adams," his mom said, getting out a pencil and making some marks on his English curriculum. "Tell me what you think she looks like."

"A . . . well, she looks like a little, er, elf," Tor said. His mom laughed again.

"Exactly," she said. "You expect her to sleep in a tree or something, right?"

"You've met all my teachers?" Tor asked cautiously.

"Snow Park is tiny," his mom said, and the gloom that had lifted from her seemed to drop around her like a cloak. She looked down at his papers again, but Tor was sure she wasn't seeing them. "I've only been here a month but I think I've met everybody. I met Beryl Petrus at the supermarket. Kaia Adams was in the library with her husband when I went there for a book. And Justin Ewald is on the community clinic board."

Suddenly the light dawned on Tor. "You might lose your job because Brian Slader died? But it wasn't your fault. He was in Denver. You weren't even taking care of him when he died."

"I know," Dr. Sinclair said. "But the truth isn't always important. Sometimes perception is more important."

Tor took a deep breath.

"Do you know about the curse? That there's some sort of curse here?" he asked. "Does it have something to do with us? Is that why this is happening?"

There was a long silence at the kitchen table, and Tor held his breath.

"I've heard rumors," his mom admitted finally. She stood up from the table and went to the kettle on the stove. "I'm going to make tea."

"Do you believe in curses?" asked Tor.

"What did I tell you about truth?" his mom asked him, looking back at him.

"Truth isn't always important," Tor said. He looked down at his math homework. Math was clean, he thought suddenly. Nobody could make two plus two equal anything but four. Ever. Truth and perception were the same in math.

"Perception can kill," Dr. Sinclair said. "I used to work with a nurse from Haiti. She was a *houngon*. That's a good voodoo queen."

Tor sat with his math book open and forgotten in front of him.

"Er?" he said finally.

"Voodoo is all about perception. The blood, the *gris-gris,* the chanting, and the music. A few drugs to help the process. People who've been cursed with voodoo often die just because they believe they're going to die. Does that make sense?"

"She was a voodoo queen?" Tor asked.

"Yes, she was, and a damned fine nurse, too," Dr. Sinclair said with a slanted sort of smile. "Don't worry, she was a good voodoo queen, and she gave most of it up. She taught me two things. The first thing she taught me was how to make real shrimp etouffee."

"That's, er, food, right?" Tor asked.

"Right," Dr. Sinclair said. "And very delicious, too."

"And the second?"

"That truth is not always as important as perception, Tor. That's why we have to worry about a curse. Not that it's real, or that curses are real. But because some people *believe* it's real," Dr. Sinclair said seriously. The teakettle started to make a whistling sound. "We'll get through this, and we won't have to leave Snow Park."

"Where would we go?" Tor asked. "If we had to go?"

"I'd have to go back to inner-city Detroit, probably," she said, her hand holding a teabag in midair. "I'd have to go back to double shifts, give me some time so I could find a job somewhere else."

"Detroit?" Tor asked, feeling the word in his mouth. Detroit might not be so bad. Maybe there were places to go snowboarding in Michigan. It snowed a lot there, right?

"Me, honey, not you," Dr. Sinclair said gently, and plopped the teabag into the hot water in her cup. Tor watched her shoulders droop as the teabag sank in the hot water. "You'd have to go back to your dad in San Diego. I couldn't take you to that area of Detroit. I'd be working all the time, too. I'd have to sleep at the hospital most nights. I couldn't leave you alone."

There was a silence in the kitchen, and the teapot hissed in a lower and lower tone, as though it were a baby dragon going back to sleep.

"I'd rather stay here," Tor said finally, after thinking of and then discarding a hundred things to say.

"Me too," Dr. Sinclair said.

Tor got up to wipe down his board for the second time and let his hands linger on the smooth glossy surface. Snowboarding was like flying, like having invisible wings. No screaming baby twins woke him up at night anymore, and he didn't have to listen to his dad and his stepmom fight all the time over money. The air smelled good here, like the ocean that he was supposed to live by since he was from California but that he rarely got to see. He liked it here with his mom, who seemed to really like having him around. He had some real friends. He wasn't going to give this up. He just wasn't.

When Tor woke up to the alarm, he groaned. Every muscle hurt, and the back of his head felt like he'd smacked it repeatedly against something very hard. Oh, that's right, he had. Worst of all, it was another school day.

Then he remembered the night before and what his mom had told him. He got out of bed and headed for the bathroom and a hot shower. He was going to figure out what the curse was. Then he was going to fix it or destroy it. He wasn't sure how, but he was going to do it.

He walked through the halls from class to class without really seeing anything. The whispers and pointing may have been worse than yesterday, but he didn't see them so he didn't care. After math class he felt rather than saw a tall form coming right at him in the hallway.

Tor had just spent the past two days learning how to balance his body on a snowboard. He found himself twisting sideways, leaning backward, and stepping to one side with a speed he didn't know he possessed.

There was a crash. A tall high schooler thudded into the bank of lockers, setting up a musical rattle of locks as they bounced against metal. He turned to Tor with a furious look on his face. Tor recognized him: he was one of the boys who'd burst into the clinic that night when Brian Slader had gotten sick.

"Hey," Tor said, keeping himself balanced and easy on his feet. He had no idea what was going to happen next, but it certainly couldn't be good.

"You waster," snarled the boy.

"Why am I a waster?" Tor asked conversationally, hearing the chatter and bustle die down as students came to a halt around them. "People keep calling me that, but no one bothers to explain why."

"You're . . . you're a waster," the boy said again. His fists clenched tightly, but he didn't throw a punch at Tor. Tor felt his heart hammering in his chest, but he kept his face relaxed and inquiring.

"We've covered that part," Tor said. "You do speak English, right? *Habla inglés?*"

A muffled snort of laughter came from the crowd that had suddenly, magically, surrounded them. There were elementary kids and high schoolers in the crowd, a mix of heights and ages that made Tor's head spin. Didn't the teachers patrol the halls, with such a range of grades and ages mixing it up in here? The snowboarder had at least a foot and two grades on Tor.

"You killed Brian," the snowboarder said. "Your mom, the doctor, she killed him."

Tor tightened his own fists at that. He couldn't help it. "The autopsy isn't back yet," he said, trying to sound as dry and clinical as his mother. "Until the drug toxicology comes back and the complete report is out, nobody knows what really happened."

The boy's jaw dropped open in what oddly looked like dismay. Suddenly another boy elbowed his way through the crowd.

"Jeff, take it easy," he said, taking the snowboarder by the elbow. "No fighting in school or you're off the team. You *know* that."

Tor felt his fists unclench a bit. He really didn't want to have a fistfight with an older student. He was going to get creamed if they fought. But he wasn't going to back down, either.

"It's the curse," somebody said in the crowd surrounding them. The whisper ran through the students in the hallway, echoing like a murmur of surf on the beach—*the curse, the curse, the curse.*

Time suddenly started up again as a teacher shouldered through the crowd. It was Mr. Ewald, Humpty Dumpty himself, with an angry look on his smooth, round face. His entire bald head was flushed, he was so upset, and the students melted away quickly.

"What's going on here? Jeff? Max?" he asked.

"Nothing, sir," Jeff said. "We were just talking."

"You, what happened here?" Mr. Ewald asked Tor.

"Nothing, sir," Tor echoed. It was the code of any school—the teachers were Authority, and you didn't snitch. Mr. Ewald's face flushed even pinker, and he flapped his small arms at them.

"Get to class. I expect better of you, Max. You too, Jeff. And—what is your name again?"

"Tor Sinclair," Tor said.

There was a pause as Mr. Ewald took a breath, held it, and let it out. His moon-shaped face showed his thoughts clearly: here was Dr. Sinclair's son, Dr. Sinclair may have caused the death of Brian Slader, therefore . . .

"Get back to class, all of you," he said in a different tone. He ignored Tor completely. He went to Max and Jeff and, putting his tiny arms around their shoulders, walked with them down the hall, speaking to them in hushed and gentle tones.

Tor turned and walked the other way, feeling a mixture of outrage and loneliness so strong his stomach churned.

At lunch Tor steeled himself and entered the cafeteria, trying to ignore the whispers and stares that followed him now more than ever. He glanced over at Raine and

Drake and felt disgusted with himself for being so grateful for their nod. He didn't need them. But he was still glad they were there.

"Bad day today, eh?" Drake said, dunking a chicken nugget into his ketchup.

"Yep," Tor said. He should have been too upset to eat, but his body overrode his mind. He'd been snowboarding hard for two days and he was going again today. He was hungry. He dug in.

"Sorry about your mom," Raine said, and Tor could have sworn she looked guilty for a moment.

"It wasn't her fault," Tor said. "It'll all come out."

"Probably not," Drake said.

"You going to tell me about this curse, or what?" Tor said, opening his chocolate milk with hands that shook slightly. He stuck the straw in and pulled at the straw so hard his cheeks sucked in.

Drake and Raine had an entire conversation with eyebrows and frowns while Tor emptied his milk carton.

"No, I really want to," Raine finally said out loud, and that ended it.

Drake turned to Tor and his voice was so low in the noise and clamor of the cafeteria that Tor had to lean in to hear.

"Raine has to tell you," Drake said. "Not me."

"Why?"

"Because she was my ancestor. My great-great-great-grandmother cursed the town," Raine said.

5 ☠ THE CURSE

TOR COMPLETELY FORGOT that he was supposed to meet Raine and Drake at the Pro Shop that afternoon. He forgot about school, he forgot about the curse, he forgot about everything. He had finally found his balance on his snowboard.

He'd promised Gloria he'd practice his falling-leaf move. This time the feeling was there, the same feeling he'd started to have the day before; the balance, the sense of knowing where his body was, and the stance on his board that made him feel like he and the board were one.

He slid fast down the slope, the air whipping by his helmet, then turned and glided across the snow. He almost came to a stop, then pointed his board downslope and immediately felt the snowboard come alive under his feet. It wanted to go downhill, it wanted to go fast, and he wanted to go fast, too.

Then another turn and glide. Tor felt a burst of pure joy. He pointed his board downslope again and rode all the way to the bottom without falling.

The third time he hopped off the chairlift he felt his muscles trembling with the effort. He was wearing out and he knew it, but he was having too much fun to stop. As he took off, something came by him so fast and so close that he lost his balance and fell. He landed hard on his backside and skidded downhill.

"Waster!" called a voice as the snowboarder curved by, throwing a long wave of snow into the air. The rider was wearing a helmet and goggles and a blue jacket. Of course. Tor panted in the snow, his elbows stinging from the impact, and then he levered himself to his feet. He started going downslope. This meant nothing. The board, the alive feel of it, the perfect balance—

Another boarding team member shot by, and this one ran right over the front of Tor's board. He heard a grinding sound and suddenly he was out of control. He realized in a panic that he was heading right for the trees. Trees were killers, he remembered frantically. Gloria had warned him to stay out of the trees, and he couldn't stop.

There was only one thing to do. Tor tried to fall down, caught an edge of his board, rotated forward, and slammed onto his face. The impact took the breath right out of him. He knew he was still falling, but he couldn't see because his face was in the snow. He tumbled, his board catching and twisting so hard his legs felt like they were going to break. He finally slowed down and came to a stop. Tor rolled over, gasping, to see bristly green tree branches not more than a foot away from him. He could smell the pine needles.

Laughter echoed on the hill. Two more snowboarders in blue coats shot by.

"Get out of Snow Park, waster!" one of them shouted, and they disappeared down the hill.

If anyone heard their laughter, thought Tor miserably, they'd think some kids were just having fun. He wiped his face slowly with his mitten and tried to get the snow out from between his goggles and helmet. There was a burning patch of cold on his belly. His coat had rucked up in the fall and his stomach was packed with icy snow. His legs were sore and aching, but nothing seemed to be broken. He spit some snow out of his mouth and it was very red. He looked at the blood on the snow with a detached sort of interest. He must have split his lip when he fell, but his face was numb and there wasn't any pain. Yet. Tor spit again and looked at the blood that spattered the snow. There was blood coming from his nose, too.

He couldn't sit here long. If he did, the snowboarding team would be back. He wondered if Jeff and Max were in that group. They couldn't come back uphill to him, but they could race to the bottom, get on the chairlift, and then come down the mountain after him. They might not stop at this; the possibility existed that they might kill him. It would be put down as an accident, of course, but that wouldn't keep Tor from being dead. They thought that Brian Slader had died because of the curse, and they hated Tor because he was a part of the curse, and he didn't even know what it *was* yet.

Tor got up. It wasn't the hardest thing he'd ever done, but it was definitely up there in the hot top five. His board tried to slip out from under his feet, his balance was gone, and he was shaky. He went down the rest of the hill like a baby taking his first steps—board forward, then heel side and stop. Board forward, then back to a stop again. Tor forgot about the snow in his goggles and helmet and the snow inside his coat. He actually started to sweat with the effort of staying upright, of making it to the bottom of the hill before his tormenters returned, of not sitting down in the snow and bursting into tears like a little kid.

Finally he reached the chairlifts. He unsnapped his boots from his snowboard. Without a backward look, his back as straight as he could make it, he walked firmly to the lodge and then through the building and down Main Street to the Pro Shop.

"Hello, Tor," Mr. Douglas said as Tor entered. "Raine said you'd be here. She's going to help with an assignment, that right?"

"That's right," Tor said. A large clump of snow slid out from under his coat and hit the floor with a plop. He propped his board against the wall. Water started dripping off his head, and he took his helmet off. More snow packed the interior. Mr. Douglas's lips twitched in concern when he glanced at Tor's face, but he didn't say a word.

"You can head on back if you'd like," Mr. Douglas said kindly.

"Could I ask a favor?"

"Sure, what do you need?"

Tor explained, and Mr. Douglas gave him a look.

"You sure?"

"Yes, sir," Tor said, and then he picked up his board and went to the back room.

"I see you got the Snow Park Swirlie," Drake observed as Tor stood in the doorway.

"Oh, look at your board," Raine said. Her mouth thinned into an angry line as she took it from his arms and examined the glossy surface.

Tor hadn't wanted to look at it. He'd heard the grinding sound, and he was afraid to see what the snowboarder had done to his beautiful board.

"You would look at the board first, wouldn't you, Raine? Look at his *face*. This was more than the usual swirlie of the new guy. They wanted to really hurt you," Drake said. He was lounging in his Sherlock Holmes chair, his books spread on his lap. Today he was wearing a sweater in contrasting and uneven stripes of muddy brown, green, and orange. The sweater was so horrible it made Tor feel better. He wasn't really sure why.

"Nicked on the edge and the surface was scraped, but I can repair that. It didn't go deep enough to touch the inner core," Raine was muttering. She got out a screwdriver and took Tor's bindings off his board while Tor stripped down to his boarding pants and his thermal underwear top.

"Here, wear this," Drake said, and threw an ancient-looking blue jersey at him. "You're freezing again."

"Just got a little wet," Tor said, shrugging into the jersey. The jersey was three sizes too big and the cuffs were frayed, but he was grateful for the warmth. The damp patch on his thermals was burning him, it was so cold. He sat down to dig snow out of his socks. In a few minutes there was a puddle of melting snow at his feet.

Raine took out a wax pencil. She sat down with his board and started working on it. She glanced up at Tor to see him looking steadily at her.

"You'd better start," Drake said, settling even more deeply into his chair. "He might get struck by lightning any minute."

Raine jumped, glared at Drake, and then laughed. But it wasn't a happy laugh.

"Okay, then," she said. "I wish this story weren't true, but it is."

"I'm ready," Tor said.

"My great-great-great-grandmother was named Leaping Water. Do you know anything about the Ute?"

"Ute?" Tor said in confusion. For a moment he thought she'd said "youth," which was a very old-fashioned word for a kid to be using. "What is a Ute?"

"Indians," Drake said, and made a quiet yelling noise while patting his hand against his mouth. "Native Americans. You heard about those?"

"Well, sure, of course. I just never heard about Utes before. You're a Ute?" Tor asked Raine.

"Couldn't you tell?" she said, pointing the waxing stick at her face.

"I thought . . . I dunno, I didn't notice," Tor confessed, and Drake gave a yelp of laughter.

"You serious?" he asked.

"So what if he didn't notice, Drake," Raine said with a sniff. "You really didn't notice?"

"We've got all sorts of colors in San Diego," Tor tried to explain. He felt bad. "Mexican Americans, lots of African Americans, Asian Americans, and don't forget all the people coming out to Hollywood to be actors, marrying each other and making all sorts of new blends. I mean, skin color in California isn't exactly, er, black and white."

"Well, I guess so," Drake said, grinning.

"I forgive you for not noticing my Native heritage," Raine said, and bent back to Tor's snowboard with her waxing stick. "You make me laugh, Tor, you really do. You truly never noticed?"

"You were nice. I never noticed anything else," Tor said, and then he had to look awkwardly into his teacup because he didn't want to see Drake laughing at him.

There was a silence, and nobody laughed. Raine stroked the snowboard with long, smooth gestures, and Tor felt oddly like she was soothing the spirit of the snowboard instead of simply repairing it. Or maybe that was because he suddenly knew she was a Ute, and now she had spiritual qualities that all Indians were supposed to have. He felt embarrassed at the thought.

"Leaping Water," Drake prompted.

"First, the Ute," Raine said. "We were people of this land before the white settlers got here, but we weren't natives here either. Our tribe's history begins through other tribes—their histories talk about driving away Utes from *their* lands. From the Apache to the Navajo, the Ute were constantly seeking a home and always being driven away."

"But where did they come from originally?"

"I think they came from Atlantis," Drake said, and Raine shot him a very dirty look.

"No one knows. Maybe my people were from Mexico, or Central America, or even some place back East. Perhaps a plague or another, stronger tribe drove them from their lands. You think of America before the Europeans as a settled place, maybe even all peaceful and stuff, but it really wasn't. There were lots of wars, and sometimes things happened that nobody can explain at all."

"The Anasazi," Drake said. "My favorite mystery story."

"You'd learn about them if you'd gone to elementary school in Colorado, Tor," Raine explained. "You would know about Utes, too, and Shoshone and Cheyenne and Arapahoe. The Anasazi were a cliff-dwelling tribe of Indians who disappeared entirely, leaving their intact villages behind. My people arrived a lot later. My people, the Utes, settled in the Colorado mountains."

"Perfect mountain people," Drake said, lazily flipping through his math book. "Always want to play, ride horses, hang out, party."

"Not exactly farming types," Raine agreed. "We were the last tribe to be located on a reservation. The Meeker Massacre took place in 1879, a long time after the Trail of Tears. Even the tribes like the Apache, and they were awesome warriors, even those tribes had surrendered before the Utes were finally moved to a reservation."

"To where?" Tor asked.

"Utah," Drake said. "That's why the state is named Utah."

Tor smacked his forehead with his hand. He hadn't made the connection, and now it was so obvious he felt like a fool.

"Why aren't you there, then?" he asked. "In Utah?

How come your great-great-great-grandmother escaped the Meeker Massacre?"

"Oh, the Meeker Massacre wasn't a massacre of Utes," Raine said with a rather pointed smile. "It was a massacre *by* the Utes. Nathan Meeker was a white man assigned to teach our people how to be farmers."

"Get off those horses, stop fooling around, and bust that sod," Drake said.

"That wouldn't fly," Tor said thoughtfully. Already he thought of the Utes as his kind of people, even though he wasn't remotely Indian.

"Nope. So they finally got tired of Meeker, and they killed him. Then they killed a bunch of U.S. Cavalry, and then finally they agreed to relocate to Utah before the entire U.S. Cavalry came back in force and wiped them all out. They knew they were beat, but they surrendered on their terms. We Utes, we were one of the few Native tribes to successfully make peace with the white man," Raine said. There was a distinct note of pride in her voice.

"But Leaping Water didn't go to Utah," Tor said. "Right?"

"She was already married to Frederick Borsh," Raine said.

"That doesn't sound very Utish," Tor said. Drake snorted and Raine grinned.

"Nope. Fred was pure German, lederhosen and

pointy Tyrolean hat and all. What a couple they must have made, eh?"

Tor blinked at the image: a Native American princess in a doeskin dress and beads, with long black braids, holding hands with a plump German man in a white shirt with suspenders, leather shorts, and big boots. It just didn't seem possible.

"Weird. So she stayed. Was the town doctor involved in this? Did she curse the town doctor because of her people being driven away?" Tor asked.

"No," Raine said. "That came much later. Now you know the background—my people were here, then they were gone, and only Leaping Water stayed behind. Here in Snow Park, which was called, I think, Cooperstown?"

"Coopersville," Drake supplied.

"Coopersville. Frederick Borsh made a mining claim here and worked a mine in the mountain next to the town. He never found gold, as far as we know, but he never gave up. Legends say he tunneled all over that mountain."

"Which mountain?" Tor asked.

"The one without any chairlifts or ski slopes, of course," said Drake, and lifted a hand as Tor started to ask another question. "Listen."

"He and Leaping Water also ran Borsh's General Store. There was a lot of racism in those days, of course, but she was such a gentle and kind little creature that

75

few people minded buying groceries from Mr. Borsh's Ute wife. Their store is still in operation. But it sells ski and boarding equipment now."

"Here in Snow Park?" Tor asked.

"Right here," Raine said with a smile, and she pointed her stick straight down at the floor. Tor felt a chill run right up his spine.

"Whoa," he said.

"After Frederick died in the 1918 flu epidemic, Leaping Water spent a lot of time on the mountain he'd worked. Some said she was looking for his ghost. She let the store pass to her daughter and her son-in-law, and she got battier and battier."

"Battier?" Tor asked.

"It was about 1950 that everything was really set in motion. Dr. Robert Malone moved here. He'd been a mountaineer in World War II, a combat skier, and a doctor, and he'd spent a lot of time skiing in the European mountains after the war. He realized we had the same snow and the same gorgeous mountains here, and he started buying up property in dying little Coopersville. He petitioned the town and the name was changed to Snow Park."

"And a winter resort was born," Drake said.

"Your great-great-great-grandmother was alive in 1950?" Tor asked in astonishment. "How old was she?"

"She was born in 1858," Raine said proudly. "So she was ninety-two in 1950. She died in 1952. I think."

"You *think*? You don't know?"

"Let her finish the story," Drake said. "Then you'll understand."

"Dr. Malone was the town mayor and the town doctor, and he offered riches and a future to the newly named Snow Park. There was only one problem with his grand plan."

"The mountain that belonged to Leaping Water," Tor said. "Ahh."

"It was perfect for the new ski development. But he couldn't get Leaping Water to sell," Raine said sadly. "She was all the way around the bend by then, a crazy old Ute talking about how 'her people' lived on that mountain and she had to protect them."

"Her people?"

"She would never explain what that meant," Raine said. She bent her head down so all Tor could see was the part in her glossy black hair. She was pretending to concentrate on the nick in his snowboard. "Of course she couldn't mean her people, the Utes. Our people are mostly on a reservation in Utah. There weren't any Utes living in the mountains around here except for Leaping Water. So people thought she must mean something crazy. How'd you like to have kids in the third grade chase you around claiming your grandmother had a thing going for Bigfoot?"

"Life can always get worse," Drake said, as though it were his own personal motto. Tor looked at him and

Drake looked down at his math book again, idly stirring the pages and refusing to look at Tor.

"So she didn't sell. Obviously, she won. There's nothing on that mountain, right?" Tor said. "Do you own it? Your family?"

"We own it."

"Why don't you live there? I mean, build a house or something?"

"Too dangerous," Drake and Raine said at the same time.

"Nobody goes on the mountain, not even my family," Raine said. "It's dense. Lots of trees. And mine shafts that my great-great-great-grandfather dug."

"So why would anyone want it?" Tor asked.

"With enough money they can bulldoze down the trees and plug up the mine shafts," Drake said.

"Now you know almost the whole story, Tor," Raine said. "Dr. Malone put all sorts of pressure on the Douglas family. That'd be my great-grandpa, James. But the mining claim belonged to Leaping Water and my family stuck with her decision, even if she was batty and all. Then one day she came down Main Street, dressed in her Ute best—I mean beaded doeskin dress, boots, her hair braided with shells and beads, her face like a crazy woman, and she cursed the mayor in front of his doctor's office. Right in front of ten witnesses. Not me, I wasn't born yet."

"Within a few years everyone in town claimed to have been there," Drake said drily.

"Doctor's office?" Tor said with a sinking feeling. "The same?"

"The same place," Drake said, "where your mom works now."

Tor remembered the pipes and lines and tunnels that he'd seen in that open manhole cover that day in San Diego, the pipes that must also run under every place in Snow Park. He gripped his empty cup in his hands and licked at his sore lip.

"Leaping Water told him she would never sell her husband's mining claim. She said that Dr. Malone was cursed; that every doctor forevermore that came to Snow Park would be cursed, that no healer could stay in Snow Park until they talked to her people and agreed to protect them. Then she turned and walked into the mountain and no one ever saw her again."

"She 'walked into the mountain'?" Tor asked. He didn't think he'd heard Raine properly.

"She was last seen walking on the road that leads to Borsh Mountain," Raine said, rubbing Tor's snowboard with an absentminded hand. The scratch that had marred it was gone. It looked as good as new. "That's the last anyone ever saw of her."

"Dr. Malone never lived to see the first chairlift take skiers up the hill," Drake said with relish. "Served him right, trying to bully an old woman like that. Besides, the town did okay without that mountain anyway, right?"

"He died?"

"He was walking out of the Denver County Courthouse two weeks later, when construction workers across the street dropped a load of stone from a scaffold. Two pieces of marble exploded like a grenade going off. A piece struck the doctor, killing him instantly. He was at the courthouse trying to get the mining claim revoked so he could take over the mountain."

"The curse had struck," Raine said. "Nobody in Snow Park could talk about anything but the curse from then on. The next doctor, Dr. Alan Victor, got a horrid cancer and died less than a year after he came here."

"Then there was that one doc—what was his name? Didn't he go to jail? He was, like, a heroin addict or something?" Drake said.

"Dr. Reginald Maclean," Raine said, as though she knew all of the names and had them written down somewhere. As though saying them hurt her. "He blew out a knee skiing and got hooked on painkillers. Then he moved on to heroin. He got caught and lost his license, and he had to go to rehab. He never came back."

"Who took over the lodge and development and stuff?" Tor asked. He turned his empty mug over and over in his hands, fiddling with it the way that Raine was fiddling with Tor's snowboard and Drake was fiddling with his math book.

"The doctor's daughter," Drake said. "Rebecca Malone Lowen. Smart woman, and she was married to a Denver attorney who liked to ski. Snow Park continued on schedule with a single break—for Dr. Malone's funeral. And no doctor has lasted in this town for more than a year ever since. Not all of them die. Some just move away. Most years we haven't had a doctor at all. The ones who come here, they don't stay."

"The curse," Tor said.

"The curse," Drake and Raine said as one, and Raine looked at him with sad eyes in the face that used to be ordinary but was forevermore exotic to Tor—a Ute face.

"You don't really believe in it, do you?" Tor asked. "The curse?" He was thinking of his mother and what she'd said about truth and perception.

"I believe it," Raine said, and shrugged. "And I don't care if you think I'm crazy. I'm the Bigfoot-loving great-great-great-granddaughter, you know."

"Crazy is in her job description," Drake said.

"You believe?" Tor asked him.

"Yes," Drake said calmly. "Yes, I do."

"I don't know if I do," Tor said, but he was lying.

"You will," Raine said.

Tor clenched his hands around his cup. "Then we'll have to fix it," he said.

"Time to get on home now, kids," Mr. Douglas said, appearing in the doorway and startling them all so they jumped. "I'm closing up and we need to get to supper before Elinor gets furious at the both of us and burns the stew. Here are your things, Tor."

Tor took the package that Mr. Douglas was holding out to him. He gave them all a grin that didn't feel straight on his face, and he showed the package to Drake and Raine. They looked at what he'd asked Mr. Douglas to get for him: a set of thermals, sized for a small woman. Sized for Dr. Sinclair.

"We're going to be here a long time," Tor said firmly. "So I thought my mom should have some of these, too."

Drake and Raine looked at him and Tor felt something very warm inside him. Mr. Douglas sighed and turned away, but his friends did not. They glanced at each other and then turned back to him.

"Here's your snowboard, Tor," Raine said.

"See you tomorrow," Drake said.

6. DEEP POWDER

"TOR, WAKE UP!" His mother was speaking to him.

Tor tried to sit up and then flopped back on the bed, groaning. His body was one big bruise and his mouth felt swollen to twice its normal size. His head throbbed in time to his heartbeat.

"School?" he mumbled. The hall light shone dimly into the room. Tor glanced at the clock. Three o'clock in the morning. His aches were forgotten as he sat upright. "Problem?"

"Don't get up," Tor's mom said. She sat on the bed, dressed warmly in her red snowsuit. Her new thermal shirt showed under the V of her scrubs. Tor tried to blink himself awake.

"I'm up," he said.

"I need to go to the clinic," Dr. Sinclair said calmly. "I don't want you to go with me this time. I was silly to make you come with me before. You're only a few blocks from me, so just stay in bed, sleep, and I'll be back before you know it. I just wanted you to know if you wake up, that's where I am."

"But I can come—"

"No," Dr. Sinclair said firmly. "I've thought about this. You're old enough to be by yourself. Go to sleep."

She pressed her hand against his chest and he lay back down reluctantly. The odd thing was, as soon as his body was back in the bed and she'd tucked his covers up to his chin, he was already half-asleep again.

"Okay," he said. "Be careful."

"I'm always careful," Dr. Sinclair said. "Thanks again for the thermals, Tor. I'm warm as toast now." She smoothed his hair, kissed his forehead, and in a moment the darkness was complete. Tor didn't even hear the front door close.

Dr. Sinclair walked down the snow-covered street toward the clinic, her big snow boots clumping along, her breath floating back from her head like a white balloon. She was carrying her black doctor's bag in one mittened hand. The lights of the clinic were on and there were people inside. They were nothing but shadows moving against the light.

The snow had been falling for several hours and there hadn't been a breath of wind. The soft, light powder was as fluffy as goose down. Puffs of snow flew up with every step she took. The few streetlights lit the underside of more snow clouds, thick and heavy, pressing down on the town and catching on the tops of the buildings.

Dr. Sinclair stopped for a moment and changed her bag from hand to hand. There was a person on the porch of the clinic, like Coach Rollins had been waiting when Brian Slader had taken sick. But this man wasn't the snowboarding coach. He was much taller, too tall to be human. Whatever it was loomed like a stick insect under the clinic porch, wrapped in darkness.

Abruptly, the thing left the porch and started loping toward her, faster than a person should have been able to run. It left no footprints in the snow and it left no cloud-breath of air behind it. Dr. Sinclair dropped her medical bag in the snow and stepped back. The creature was right in front of her. The face was pale and remote as snow crystals, and the blood that rimmed its mouth was as red and damp as a fresh rose petal. As it reached for her, Dr. Sinclair began to scream.

Tor sat up in his bed, gasping, his hands beating in the air in front of him like he was caught in spiderwebs. He looked around wildly, but there were no vampires in his room. His heart hammered and his mouth tasted hot and dry and horrible.

He looked at the clock. Three-ten. His mom had left only minutes ago. He could catch her, save her, if he was quick. He threw off his warm blankets and pulled his snowboarding pants over his pajamas.

He was pulling his hat on his head as he shoved his feet into his boots. Then he was out the door, shrugging into his coat, his mittens clutched in his hands. The door slammed behind him, and he was plunged into cold darkness as though he'd just jumped into icy water.

The town lay before him, muffled in snow so that every edge was softened and every line was blurred. The hanging stoplight on the main intersection was covered with snow. It was lit up like a glass globe with a blinking amber light inside.

The heavy clouds that meant more snow pressed down on the tops of the buildings, near enough that Tor felt like he could leap into the air and grab the cloud, rip it open, and send snow cascading out.

His mother was nowhere to be seen. Her footprints left neat stitches in the snow. Tor ran down the street following the trail, dreading to find their end, careless of the whistling and panicked breath he was making. He pulled his mittens on as he ran, and then he skidded to a stop.

The footprints disappeared into the Snow Park Clinic, and he saw his mother behind the glass. For a moment all Tor could do was stand and watch her, her hair like a curly halo around her head, her face so serious and so kind.

Dr. Sinclair was bending over a little girl and sticking

what looked like a white tube in the girl's mouth. Two adults were standing inside the clinic, clutching each other, staring at Dr. Sinclair and the little girl. The girl heaved a big breath, her shoulders rising and falling, and the couple broke into a silent pantomime of grateful tears.

An asthma attack. That was what Tor was watching. He was watching his mother save a little girl from an asthma attack. There was no white-faced vampire waiting to kill her.

The nightmare tore into tatters around him. Tor felt, in its place, an overwhelming wave of embarrassment. He couldn't let his mother know he'd followed her. He thought she was being attacked by a *vampire*? It would be too humiliating if she found out. He took two careful steps back, keeping his eye on the clinic, afraid that they would see him standing in the snow.

A few flakes of new snow spiraled by Tor's head and then a few more. Then the air was full of snow, perfect little crystals that caught in his hair and eyelashes and started covering his arms and shoulders. The clouds had finally broken open and the snow was going to come in earnest now.

Tor stopped and stood still, surrounded by a dream-like swirl of falling snowflakes. There was something he was missing, he realized, something his dream was trying to tell him. Why would he have a nightmare about vampires?

Then he had it, as suddenly as that. The two snowboarders that he'd overheard in the hallway at school, they'd talked about a "he" that was making them do something. Something was going on with the snowboarding team, and Brian Slader had been part of the team. Brian had suddenly gotten sick, and then he had died.

Everyone had blamed his mother for Brian Slader's death because of the curse. The snowboarders who were tormenting him, the townspeople, they all believed in the curse.

But what if the curse *wasn't* the reason Brian had died? What if there was somebody else, like his dream vampire, who was responsible for Brian's death? If that was true, it was all too easy to put the blame on the old town curse. Dr. Sinclair would get the blame and the killer would get away.

Tor took step after careful step away from the clinic and finally turned and ran for home. His mind was full of thoughts that stayed with him all the way back into the house and into his bed. It was still warm.

Tor finally had an answer that made sense. Someone was covering up something. His mother hadn't killed Brian Slader by accident. Someone had murdered him.

"No way," Drake hissed. They were leaning over their lunches, hunched like conspirators. Tor was starving, so he tried to explain his theory between enormous bites of Tater-Tot casserole.

"Why would someone murder Brian?" Raine asked, her forehead puckered in distress. "There'd be no reason."

"Maybe it was an accident," Tor said. He held up his hand at Raine's increased look of distress. "Or maybe he was murdered. It doesn't matter, because now this person is *using* the curse, to try and make people think it's all my mom's fault. My mom calls it perception, and it can be more important than the truth."

"There's only one thing," Drake said, sucking the last of his milk through a straw. "You still haven't answered *why.*"

"I don't know why," Tor said, and forked up the last of his vegetables from his tray. They weren't very appetizing, but he was still hungry. "That's what I have to find out. Why would Brian lose so much blood? Is there some drug that does that?"

"I don't know," Drake said. "The coach, Coach Rollins, he's tough. He's the deputy sheriff, too, you know. He's a great rider, not as good as my dad, but he's really good. And he's tough. He wouldn't let them do, you know, drugs."

"I know," Tor said, thinking of the deputy's hard handshake and equally hard grin.

"The kids on the team are randomly tested for drugs," Drake said. "That's standard. So they couldn't have been doing drugs. They're clean."

"Then there must be something else," Tor said, looking at his completely empty tray.

"There's always the curse," Drake said unhelpfully.

"First things first," Tor said. "First I figure out who's trying to set up my mom to take the fall for Brian Slader. Then we solve the curse. The real curse."

"Oh, so no problem, then," Drake said.

"I do like your attitude, Tor," Raine said.

"Not so much in the brains department, but plenty of attitude," Drake said with a cynical pointed smile.

"You'll have to provide the brains, then, Drake," Tor said. He hunched forward over his empty plate. "We can do this, you know. Figure it all out. Fix it. I know we can."

Raine opened her mouth as if to say something, then closed it. Finally she shrugged. "It's worth a try," she said. "At least I won't be moping around thinking that something horrible is going to happen to your mom and it's all my family's fault."

"We're going to make sure nothing else happens," Tor said. He knew he was doing some more of the attitude thing, but he couldn't help himself.

"I'm in," Drake said. "Why not?"

"I'll be the historian. Keeper of the Curse," Raine said. "Maybe I can find something from my grandma about Leaping Water. I was too embarrassed to really ask before."

"That would really help," Tor said.

"Come by the shop after lessons," Raine said as they got up and gathered their lunch trays. "We'll plan."

"We'll plot. I like the sound of that," Drake smirked. "Plot."

"I'll be there," Tor said, and tried not to show how relieved he was. He couldn't figure out much of anything on his own, but with Drake and Raine? Together, the three of them just might have a chance.

He had friends, Tor thought as they stacked their lunch trays and headed for class. He finally had some real friends.

But unless he figured out who was trying to get his mom fired, and unless he somehow broke the ancient Ute curse, he was going to end up in some other cafeteria next year. Alone.

7 ☠ BULLDOZERS

GLORIA WAS WAITING for him after school, her yellow daisy board crusted with powder, her apple cheeks shining. "I've been riding powder all day," she said cheerfully. "You're going to love this!"

"There's so many people," Tor said, as he strapped in and got ready to slide toward the chairlift line.

"There's a race in about an hour," Gloria said. "Boardercross. I love that event. You should stay and watch, too."

"What's boardercross?" Tor asked as he and Gloria inched their way up to the front of the chairlift line.

"A snowboard competition, where four to six riders navigate through jumps and banked turns and race to the finish line. It's a lot like motorcycle motocross. There's other events, too, like the giant slalom and the half-pipe." Gloria hopped on the chairlift as it swept up to them. "Boardercross is wicked fun to watch."

"Do you compete?" Tor asked curiously.

"No way," Gloria said with a snort. "I don't like that whole competition thing. Too easy to forget what riding is all about."

"So who's riding in the race today?" Tor asked, but he already knew the answer.

"High school riders," Gloria said. "The Snow Park team has two in the finals. Look for them, they're wearing—"

"Blue coats, I know," Tor said with resignation.

"Boardercross is fun but I like half-pipe more," Gloria said. "More art, less jabbing with the elbows. Let's get a couple of runs in and then you can watch the race. Sound good?"

Tor glanced back down the mountain as the chairlift moved them toward the top of the slope. The green trees were totally white and the sky pressed down, gray as yesterday with the promise of more snow. A steady stream of people were coming through the lodge and heading toward a part of the mountain that he hadn't explored yet. Suddenly rock music started to thump, and he caught a glimpse of speakers and snapping flags and bright spotlights as the chairlift crested the hill.

When he got off the chairlift, Tor slid and fell into an ungainly tumble of arms and snowboard. He did a sort of crushed-bug crawl to a safe spot, and turned to strap in his free leg.

"You'll get it," Gloria said, standing effortlessly in her board and adjusting the chin strap of her helmet. "It just takes time. You've got the heart, that's for sure."

Tor got up and the board came alive under his feet. He let it take him for a moment, allowing a feeling he couldn't name rise up in him like a fountain. He pushed out his left heel and the board came sliding to a stop, throwing up a small curve of sparkling powder.

"Sweet," Gloria said. "One time down falling-leaf style, and then we practice the toe-side. Let's go!"

They went, and everything Tor was and everything he thought fell away and was gone. The only thing that remained was speed, the wind whipping at his cheeks, the cold of the snow, and the feel of his board in fresh powder.

When they finished the run and got back into the chairlift line, Tor could feel his cheeks stinging with the cold. He grinned at Gloria, and she grinned back and gave a little whoop and a hop, scattering snow from her board in a puff of white.

"Now it's toe-side time. That means you have to turn your back to the abyss."

"A-whatsis?" Tor said, and Gloria laughed merrily.

"The downhill slope. There's nothing harder than turning your back to the downhill slope. You'll do fine. You've got plenty of courage and that's what it takes."

Tor could feel his face flushing. Did Glorious Gloria just tell him he had courage? She must have caught his look because she reached out and jabbed him in the ribs.

"Yeah, I said courage. You keep getting up, like somebody forgot to put an off switch on you. Now don't fall off the chairlift this time."

This time, astonishingly, Tor didn't fall. He slid to a stop, upright, with such an expression of awe in his face that Gloria started laughing, lost her balance, and fell down. She hooked her free leg into her board, still laughing, rose to her feet, and gestured for him to follow.

Tor understood what Gloria meant about the abyss when she showed him toe-side riding. He had to turn his board into the mountain on his toes and turn his back to the empty air and the long fall down. He didn't think, he just did it.

Gloria raced next to him, her red coat nearly covered with white. Tor realized it had started snowing hard.

"You did it, first time!" Gloria said. "Now we connect the two—watch me."

Later, covered with snow, legs trembling, still panting but with a glow of happiness like a warm ball inside him, Tor edged his way into the crowd surrounding the boardercross slope. Gloria hadn't needed to show him the way. He'd just followed the people. The whole town was there, and all the tourists, too, it seemed. He'd left his snowboard behind at the lodge, but he was still wearing his gear. His nose and cheeks were a little cold, but the rest of him was warm as toast.

Tor edged by a round man in a canary-yellow coat and realized it was Justin Ewald, the math teacher. Mr. Ewald saw him but didn't say anything; he turned away as though he hadn't seen Tor. Tor's cheeks started heating up as others saw him and turned away—kids from school, other teachers, people he didn't know but who seemed to recognize him. Tor stepped around a tall pole covered with flags and came face to face with a man in a sheriff's uniform. This wasn't Deputy Rollins, but an older, bigger man with a face as sad and droopy as a basset hound. This had to be Sheriff Hartman.

"Er, hello," Tor said, but he couldn't hear his own voice over the pounding music and the roar of the crowd.

The sheriff nodded, said something that Tor couldn't hear, and walked on. At least he didn't look angry with Tor, or disgusted. He just looked sad.

There was a gasp and a cheer from the crowd up ahead of him but he couldn't see why. Then he heard a burst of applause. The race must have started. Tor elbowed his way through gaps and scrambled up a slope of snow where there were fewer people, finally coming to a section of orange plastic fencing that marked off the race area. Tor sat in the snow next to the fence and hunched forward, hoping no one noticed him.

Suddenly four riders shot by him, going so fast he felt like they'd sucked the breath right out of him. He turned to see them flying over a big bump in the racecourse. In midair one rider lost his balance and Tor could see he wasn't going to land properly. The rider came down in a tumble and slid into another section of plastic fencing. The other riders kept going, their elbows held tightly to their bodies and their legs bent almost double. Each time they went over a bump, everything seemed to slow down as they floated in the air, their bodies small and tight against their boards.

Tor could see the finish line, and the three riders that were left streaked across it. A cheer went up from the crowd.

The rider that had fallen regained his feet and finished the race, carefully holding his arm across his chest. Tor wondered if it was broken.

There was the sound of a distant buzzer up the mountain. Tor turned, but he couldn't see anything. The steep slope of the racecourse blocked his view. He could hear cheers and applause coming down toward him, so he knew the riders were going to appear soon.

This set of riders had a blue coat among them. The hometown crowd roared as they cheered on their favorite. The Snow Park snowboarder was breathtaking as he swept around a curve and came up to the jump that had injured the previous rider. The other four snowboarders weren't as low to the board and they weren't as controlled. Tor knew what kind of power it took to keep that low crouch over the board, when your legs felt like they were gasping for breath instead of your lungs.

The Snow Park rider came in second by the tip of his snowboard, and all the riders came to a stop and leaned over their boards, panting hard. Tor saw Coach Rollins step forward and lean over to speak to his rider. The coach had a pleasant enough look on his face, but Tor could see his fingers digging into the rider's blue coat, and the boy bowed his head. Tor felt bad for him, and then realized with a shock that the boy was Jeff Malone.

Jeff skated away from the finish line and ducked under the ropes that held back the onlookers. Tor saw Mayor Malone step forward to talk to his son, but Jeff turned away from his father and disappeared into the crowd.

Everyone was already looking up the mountain, waiting for the next team to come across the finish line. When these riders swept across the finish line with a Snow Park boarder in first place, the crowd cheered and shouted as though this meant a gold medal in the Olympics. Tor saw Coach Rollins step forward, a smile on his hard face, and he turned away.

Tor couldn't help loving the power and grace of the race. He wanted to be able to ride that way, to fly off the edge of a bump and float in the air like gravity had been suspended for a few seconds. Maybe Coach Rollins was a winning coach because he was so tough on his team. Maybe they won lots of trophies.

But if winning turned riders into mean kids who enjoyed shoving younger kids into lockers, it wasn't worth it. If winning meant that everyone who didn't win was treated like a loser, it wasn't worth it.

Tor scrambled downslope and through the crowd as the last boardercross group raced down the mountain. He didn't feel like listening to the cheers for the Snow Park snowboarding team anymore.

"First powder day?" Mr. Douglas said with a grin as Tor let the door of the Pro Shop shut behind him.

"Yeah," Tor said. Mr. Douglas was writing up a ticket and he waved a hand at Tor to go on to the back of the shop.

Drake and Raine were in their usual spots. This time Raine was working on a small forest of yellow, blue, red, and purple skis that were stacked in the corner, taking one at a time and running them along the waxing machine. The machine roared and the smell of wax filled the air. Drake was writing down algebra problems with one leg flung over the arm of his Sherlock Holmes chair. He pointed without looking up, and Tor saw a towel over the chair he was beginning to think of as his. By the time he'd brushed the last of the snow from his pants, hung up his jacket, pulled on the ancient jersey that also waited for him, and was collecting a cup of tea, Raine was finished with the waxing machine. She turned it off and everyone sighed as one.

There was a silence that was oddly comfortable, and Tor let the tea fill his insides with warmth.

"We just got some bad news," Drake said, finishing a final problem and slamming the book shut.

"Maybe this will break the curse," Raine said. "You never know."

"What news?" Tor asked.

"My great-great-great-grandparents' mining claim," Raine said. "My dad told me after school today. Mayor Malone finally got a court hearing date down in Denver for the claim. Since the original claim filing was lost, and the copy that my great-great-great-grandmother held can't be found, there's going to be a hearing to disinherit the claim and return the land to National Forest."

"Wait—disinherit? What does that mean?" Tor asked.

"Just what it sounds like," Drake said gloomily. He shifted in his chair and laid his book aside. "The original court filing of the claim was lost."

"But if it's returned to National Forest, won't that mean it'll still be protected?" Tor asked.

"Not exactly," Drake said. "National Forest can be logged, it can be mined, and it can be developed for general use that doesn't destroy the forest, such as—"

"A ski resort," Tor finished. "I see. But your mining

claim, doesn't it still mean something even if it was lost?"

"It was stolen from the government files," Raine said darkly. "That's what my dad says. We pay the taxes on the claim every year—they're really low, so it's no big deal—but unless we find the original deed, we can't keep the mayor from having the claim revoked."

"Raine," Drake said impatiently. "I bet Tor doesn't even know what a filing claim is."

"That'd be right," Tor said.

"Explain," Raine said, and flapped a hand at Drake.

"Back during the Gold Rush, when a miner found gold, or thought he found gold, he'd take his claim down to the Claim Stake Office," Drake said. "Just about every town had one, back in the 1800s, and they would file your claim on a map. If someone else had already claimed that land, you wouldn't get the claim. But like a big Monopoly board, if the place was empty, the land was yours as long as you held the claim and paid the yearly taxes."

"The office would keep a copy of the claim, of course," Tor said, emptying his teacup and stifling a longing for a hamburger.

"And the miner would get a certificate for the claim," Drake continued. "Now everyone in the town knew that the Borsh family, later the Douglas family, held the claim. So even though the filed claim was stolen and the original claim is missing—"

"What—the certificate your family got is missing?" Tor asked.

"Disappeared," Raine said. One of her black braids slipped over her shoulder and dangled down the front of her shirt. She flipped it back curtly. "And you can guess with whom."

"Leaping Water?"

"She disappeared into the mountain with the claim," Raine said.

"They're going to turn that mountain into another ski slope," Drake said. "That was against everything your great-great-great-grandmother—"

"Went crazy for," Raine finished. "That mountain is everything that makes my family a set of . . . set of . . . freaks around here. Oh, it isn't enough that we're Utes. No, we have to have a crazy squaw ancestor who curses the town so we can't keep a doctor around—"

"Maybe we can fix that part—" Tor said, but Raine kept on going as though she didn't hear him.

"Protecting some mythical people that no one has ever seen, nattering on, and now her great-great-great-granddaughter gets teased about a love affair with Bigfoot. I'm sick of it!" Raine threw her wax stick across the room and it shattered on the floor. There was a silence and Raine looked stricken.

"So, Tor, the newest Mayor Malone, he's the great-grandson of the original Dr. Malone. He's gotten a hearing in front of a sympathetic judge," Drake said calmly, getting to his feet and walking over to the shattered wax stick. He crouched down and began picking up the tiny pieces and collecting them in his palm. "Everything is connected here, isn't it? The only thing that really protected that claim was the fact that so many people knew the Douglas family and knew the story, and didn't think it was right to go against the family's wishes."

Tor thought again of his glimpse down the manhole cover in the street that day in San Diego. Tunnels and wires running everywhere under his feet, invisible.

"But now they don't care anymore," Raine said. The angry expression came back over her face. "And I don't care, either. Maybe the curse will be broken forever now."

"Oh, sure, that makes sense," Drake said, dropping the remains of the stick into the trash and taking his seat again. "Leaping Water curses the town, terrible things happen to every doctor since, up to and including Tor's mom, and now they're going to bulldoze her mountain. I'm *sure* that nothing bad will happen now."

Tor felt like someone had just put snow down his jersey. This didn't sound good at all. Drake looked surprisingly grim and pale. He was joking like he usually did, but his eyes didn't look like they were part of the joke.

"An earthquake, maybe?" Raine said in a low voice. "Or something even worse? What could be worse?"

"Flood. Fire. Plague. There's always something worse," Drake said.

"What happened? Why did this happen now?" Tor asked.

"Time, that's all that happened. I guess the grown-ups decided that the curse couldn't possibly be real—we've just had a run of bad luck with doctors. Or maybe they really think developing the mountain will break the curse and make it go away," Raine said. "Who knows what grown-ups really think?"

"Plus there's all that money everybody will make if we have another mountain with ski runs all over it. If Raine's great-great-great-grandmother doesn't come walking out of those woods with the original claim certificate, that mountain is going to be disinherited. It'll be developed by next summer," Drake said.

"And you and your mom will be long gone," Raine said. "Or we all will, because something utterly horrible is going to happen."

"Of course something horrible is going to happen," Tor said. "Mayor Malone is going to steal your land from you. That sounds typical, doesn't it? The white guys stealing the land from the Indians again? It's just not right."

Raine laughed. Tor looked over at her and she was smiling. The angry spots of color were still in her cheeks but she looked better.

"I never thought of it that way, but I guess you're right," she said. "I honestly never thought about the money. Dad would never sell, and Mom wouldn't hear of it, either. So it isn't about the money. It's about the land being developed at all."

"Because of your great-great-great-grandmother's mythical people," Tor said. "Because of her wishes. And the curse."

"Yeah," Raine said sadly.

"Well, there's one good thing," Tor said.

"What's that?" Drake and Raine said together.

"I'm not the only one facing the curse," Tor said. "We're all in it together now."

Later, Tor walked home through the freezing cold darkness and tried to keep the warmth he'd built up inside his body. He shifted his board into his other hand and thought about all the things they'd talked about. He was thinking about Mayor Malone and his plans to bulldoze Leaping Water's sacred mountain when he walked through his back door. He saw his mom struggling with Mayor Malone, who had his hands wrapped around her throat.

8. OUTRACED

"HEY!" TOR SHOUTED. He stepped forward and rammed the end of his snowboard into Mayor Malone's middle. Mayor Malone doubled over, staggered back, and sprawled on his backside on the kitchen tiles. His mouth made an O under the mustache, making the mayor look more than ever like a big Mr. Potato Head. His expensive camel-colored coat puddled around him on the floor.

"Tor!" his mom said breathlessly, and turned to the mayor, who was sitting, making a whistling sound through his open mouth. "Are you all right?"

Tor knew that sound—he'd had the air knocked out of him before, when he'd fallen off the monkey bars at school and landed flat on his back. Until the air had started coming back, all Tor could think about was trying to breathe and not being able to. He'd made the same whistling sound.

"Are you all right, Mom?" Tor said. "Did he hurt you?"

"No!" his mom said, and then, impossibly, she put her hands over her face and started to laugh. "I'm so sorry, Stanford." She didn't sound sorry at all.

"He was trying to kill you!" Tor said. The reaction was setting in as his heart slowed down. He felt sick to his stomach and furiously angry.

The kitchen was warm with light and full of good smells from something Dr. Sinclair had been cooking. Tor saw two cups of coffee sitting on the blue countertop. His mom was wearing her purple scrubs. Her cheeks had two spots of red and her eyes glittered fiercely.

"He was trying to kiss me," Dr. Sinclair said tartly. "And I wasn't prepared for it. Stanford, let me help you up. Come on, now, you're all right."

Mayor Malone was breathing again, although his face was grayish-green and sweaty. He looked at Tor with an expression so murderous that Tor tightened his grip on his snowboard and took a step back.

"I thought you were hurting my mom," he said, and there was no apology in his voice because he wasn't about to apologize. No way.

"I wouldn't hurt anyone," Mayor Malone said weakly, holding a hand over his stomach. "You didn't have the right to do that. You—"

"Actually, you know, he did," Dr. Sinclair said. "He was protecting his mother from what he thought was an attack. Next time you want to kiss me, Stanford, why don't you ask me out on a date first?" Tor felt his stomach twist as his mother laughed in a sparkling kind of way and laid a gentle hand on Mayor Malone's arm. The mayor's expression lightened a bit and he smiled down at her. She smiled back up at him, squeezed his arm, and pushed him gently toward the door. "Now, I have to put out supper for my son and me, so you need to head on home. Call me next time, all right?"

"I'll do that," Mayor Malone said. Tor thought for sure that he was going to say something to him, but he must have had second thoughts, because the mayor turned and, with a mumbled good-bye, left.

Tor went to put his snowboard away and strip out of his clothes. He felt sick. If his mom was going to go on dates with that disgusting mayor, he guessed he'd rather go back and live with his dad and stepmom. The twins would have to learn how to sleep through the night sometime, after all. He felt sicker and more upset by the second.

Dr. Sinclair was busy in the kitchen. When Tor came out of the bedroom, dressed in sweatpants and a sweatshirt, she had a supper on the table that smelled delicious. The blinds were closed on every window and that made the kitchen warmer than before.

"Hold still," his mother said. "Don't sit down." She

walked over and hugged him fiercely. "That's for saving me from that creep."

Tor felt as though something dropped through his stomach, out the bottom of his feet, and was gone. He looked at his mom and she was smiling at him even though her eyes were shiny with anger.

"Really?"

"Really. I've never been so surprised in all my life. One minute we're talking about plans for expanding the clinic and he's telling me all about this new ski area he's going to build—"

"Yeah, I know about—"

"And the next second, he's got his beef-wad arms around me and he's trying to kiss me. I think he was trying to cup my face in his hands, that's why you thought he was strangling me. What a pompous, egotistical, ridiculous jerk!"

Tor sat down, feeling cheerful and lighter than air and suddenly starving. His mother had made two individual potpies. He blew on a forkful of food and took a bite.

"So he just thought he'd mash on you, just like that?" Tor asked after he swallowed.

"Is that what they call it now?" his mom said, then shrugged and dropped into her seat as though she were a teenager. "Yeah, I guess so. He was trying to mash. Echh."

"Totally echh," Tor said, and forked another bite. "I don't remember you cooking this good."

"I didn't used to," his mom said, pulling her own potpie toward her. "I learned during medical school. Cooking was something to distract me from work. It helped me get through, I guess."

"Lots of alone time," Tor said, and took another huge bite. "I know what you mean."

There was a silence and he and his mom looked at each other. Then Tor deliberately shrugged his shoulders. Whatever had been was over now. His mom nodded as though he'd spoken, and they ate together in complete harmony, the kitchen warm and close around the two of them and the blinds closed to the snow and the night.

"Ewww," Raine said, and giggled.

"Echh is right," Drake said. "What a waster."

Today's lunch was chicken nuggets again, a sorry bit of food compared with last night's dinner, but Tor was starving. Gloria had given him another day alone to practice heel-and-toe on his snowboard and he couldn't wait for school to end so he could get to the mountain. There was even more powder today, and it was Thursday. The coming weekend would give him a chance to practice everything he'd learned. Now, though, was an opportunity to share his news about the mayor.

"I thought he was married," Tor said. "Isn't his son Jeff Malone?"

"Divorced a long time ago."

"No, I thought he was widowed," Raine corrected Drake. "Right?"

"Great small-town gossips we're turning out to be," Drake said. "We're supposed to know everything in this town. We don't know anything."

"But now you know that Mayor Malone has the hots for my mom," Tor said.

They all paused to say "Echh" again.

"That might take him off your list of suspects, Tor," Raine pointed out. "After all, if he likes her, he'd want to keep her around. He wouldn't want her gone."

Drake looked at Raine with an expression that seemed to hurt him. She looked back at Drake and winced.

"What do you mean?" Tor asked Drake, even though Drake hadn't spoken aloud.

"My father doesn't keep women around," Drake explained, with an uncaring expression that didn't reach his eyes. "They come, they go. Mayor Malone probably doesn't want to marry your mom; he just wants to, you know, sleep with her."

Tor shoved away his tray, this time with uneaten food still on it.

"Your mom?" he asked Drake. It seemed odd he hadn't asked before now.

"Dunno," Drake said with a twisted sort of smile. "I was dropped off at my dad's place at the age of three with a note attached to my overalls."

Raine stirred the uneaten food on her tray. "Drake's mom hasn't ever been seen and nobody knows who she is, but Drake's dad took him in and took care of him. Sorta."

"Sorta," Drake said. "As long as I clear out when he brings home somebody new, that is."

"Sorry about that," Tor mumbled, not knowing what else to say.

"That's okay, the girls never last more than a week," Drake said. "Raine's family lets me stay with them, those times. So you see, you stumbled into the freak-show area of your new school, Tor. Ute Girl and Sweater Boy. Sure you want to stick around?"

Tor thought about this for a moment. "I'm cursed," he pointed out.

"He's right," Raine said. She was looking at Drake with an anxious, sad expression. These two weren't just friends—they'd grown up together in a way Tor hadn't known about until now. "He has to stick with us freaks."

"Besides, people *like* you," Tor said. Oddly enough, this was true. Drake and Raine didn't care about being popular, but everyone seemed to like them. If they were freaks, they were popular freaks. "The most exclusive club in school, and I got in just by being cursed to a horrible death."

"A fair exchange," Drake said, his tense body relaxing. He grinned at Tor as he gathered his tray. "See you in choir practice, O Cursed One."

"If I make it there alive, you will," Tor said with mock gloom.

Tor felt energized as he walked out of choir at three o'clock. Ms. Adams had them sing the "Angels We Have Heard on High" song they'd been working on all week with all the parts put together: baritone, soprano, alto, and bass. Ms. Adams was wearing dark red pants and a velvety tunic in the same color. Her fiery hair looked like orange flames above the red, and she directed with such intensity that Tor found himself singing loudly for the first time.

Afterward, when she ended the piece and put down her wand, the class erupted into applause. She grinned at them, and her smile made her look more like an elf than ever. Then she threw out her arms and bowed. The bell rang amid the laughter and applause, and the school day was over.

Tor left with the song still inside his head. He smiled all the way home. There was a mountain to conquer and an abyss to face. As he bounded through the back door of his house and grabbed his thermals from the drying rack in the laundry room, he could feel happiness filling him like a water balloon. Time to ride.

* * *

On Friday afternoon, out of breath, knowing he was too tired but having too much fun to stop, Tor came to a halt halfway down the mountain as he saw the red jackets of the Ski Patrol unreeling red plastic fencing around the bottom part of the bunny slope. He sat down next to the tree line so he could watch what was going on—it looked like the chairlifts had been stopped, too. Then he heard a distant thumping sound and he understood. They were clearing a space for a Flight for Life helicopter. He hadn't seen anyone get hurt, but he'd only been riding one slope of a ski resort that covered three different mountains. Maybe that was why none of the snowboarding team had bothered him today.

The resort would cover four mountains after this summer, he suddenly thought. What would the spirit of Leaping Water do when her beloved mountain was bulldozed and groomed and turned into a playground for winter sports? Would there be an earthquake, like Raine had suggested? Or perhaps Drake was right, and there would be a fire. Or plague. Somehow they had to stop it, and he still had no idea how.

Tor propped his elbows on his knees, his board resting in the snow, and watched as the helicopter landed and three tall red-coated figures and one tiny one came out of the lodge with a sled that held a carefully wrapped patient. The tiny figure in charge was his mom, and Tor smiled as he saw her directing everyone else around her. He knew his mom loved being a doctor. The way her face lit up from the inside when she was talking about patients. The way she took charge. Her anger when Brian Slader died.

Tor waited until the helicopter took off and the plastic fencing was removed and the chairlift whirred and rumbled to life again, and then he picked himself up and made his way to the bottom of the mountain. He'd ride down the mountain one more time, because he nearly had that arc of movement that looked like a cat swishing its tail, and then he'd quit and go home. He got onto the chairlift, thinking hard, and let it take him up the mountain.

He didn't want to go back to San Diego, where the most important part of his dad's life was selling the next big house to the next big client, and the beach was a promise that never quite happened. He didn't want to live in a place where there were so many people nobody knew each other at all. He wanted to stay here, in Snow Park. He felt like he'd been waiting his whole life to come here and never knew it.

Tor strapped in after exiting the chairlift—he was managing nearly three in four exits now without crashing—and had just stood up when something slammed into his chest and lifted him off his feet and sent him backward into the snow. He hit hard on his back and didn't realize what had happened until he heard loud, ugly laughter. Tor painfully raised his head to see Jeff Malone high-fiving his friend Max. They were wearing their blue snowboarding team coats. Tor watched, admiring despite himself, as Jeff shot down the slope, angled his board up against a snowbank, and did a twisting leap in the air. He came back down, whooped in delight, and he and Max disappeared down the mountain.

"They should stick to their own side," someone sniffed, and Tor turned his head to see an angry-looking dad in skis holding a tiny tot on a leash. The tot was so muffled in a yellow snowsuit, goggles, and helmet that Tor couldn't tell if it was a boy or a girl. The tot yanked at the leash and crouched down, feet angled in a skier's snowplow, obviously dying to get going.

"Let's go, Dad!"

"In a minute, Morgan," the dad said. "Let's let those teenagers get downslope first. They're way too advanced to be on this side of the mountain," he said, more to himself than anyone else. "If I see them again, I'm calling the patrol."

Good, thought Tor as he levered himself to his feet. He didn't tell the man that he knew why Jeff and Max were on the gentle learners' slope. They were after him.

Tor stood as the father and his child carefully skied away from him. He knew who was waiting for him beyond the curve of trees, and he couldn't wait here forever as though he was scared. But there was no point in trying to face them, either. He just wasn't good enough to outrace them.

He looked around, wondering if there was another way down the mountain, and saw the other, smaller chairlift that went farther up the slope. Gloria had shown him the map of the resort as they'd gone up in the chairlifts the first day, so Tor knew the second chairlift led to something called Lucky Charms. Gloria had explained to him what a bowl was—a huge open slope, usually at the top of a mountain, cupped so that it resembled a bowl and containing some great riding at the most difficult levels.

He'd be slaughtered if he tried to ride down Lucky Charms, but it looked like there was another, gentler slope that led down under the chairlifts. If he took the chairlift up and carefully made his way right back down under the chairlifts, he was sure that Max and Jeff would give up and go somewhere else by the time he got back to the beginner's slope. Tor decided he'd try it and sat down to unhook one foot from his board so he could slide over to the other lift.

He had second thoughts after he was on the lift, as his chair climbed toward the top of the mountain. It looked pretty steep. The snow was taking a break, but the clouds looked heavy with the promise of more. Tor wondered if the chairlift would carry him right into the thick clouds. Finally the end of the lift came into sight and below him Tor saw a group of snowboarders all sitting in the snow. They were all watching something downhill. He turned in the chair and saw a terrain park to his right. The terrain park was an area that looked like a snow-covered version of a skaters' park; there were railings poking out of the snow and a series of huge bumps. As Tor watched, a rider came flying over a bump. The snowboarder twisted in midair and landed, snow flying in an arc from his board as he skidded to a stop.

The group of snowboarders clapped and applauded, and Tor saw another one get to his feet. He started sliding into the terrain park and suddenly Tor realized he was about to miss the chairlift exit.

He fell, of course. Crawling away, he realized no one else was falling as they got off the chairlift. The sense that he wasn't in the right place grew. He sat for a moment and looked over the curving edge of the bowl that was named Lucky Charms. This part of the mountain was enormous, dotted with skiers and snowboarders and covered in white snow. There wasn't a single tree in the whole bowl. Tor could see at the bottom of the bowl how different trails led to two other chairlifts, which headed toward other mountain slopes in the distance.

Only one mountain had nothing on it but trees; only one mountain was untouched—Raine's mountain. The chairlift he had just ridden was right next to the silent, snow-covered trees of her family land. The mountain was so huge and so silent next to the busy slopes of the ski resort that Tor felt as though it were looking at him.

Or maybe something was looking at him out of the darkness among the trees.

Tor stopped a shiver before it began. It was time to make his way down the hill. He stood and then sat right back down again. The slope below him looked vertical, as though he was trying to snowboard down the side of a white building. He stood up again and immediately turned into the falling-leaf stance, but he started going far too fast. Finally he managed to slow himself and stopped, trembling. He realized he was really in trouble.

"I can do this," he said to himself, and pushed his board forward.

As he started sliding down, he heard a shout behind him and knew instantly that he was caught. He'd made his way all the way up here only to be caught by Max and Jeff, and this time they were going to wreck him so badly he'd never be able to get to his feet again. Tor felt his stomach drop.

He was already going way too fast. He hadn't been careful enough, and as he tried to turn into the mountain he realized he wasn't going to be able to stop. His board rocketed across the slope of the mountain, climbed a lip of snow, and shot into space. Tor came down on the other side, and he was in the trees of Borsh Mountain, thick and green, and he was still going too fast. Tor was out of bounds and out of control and he couldn't stop.

9 ☠ THE RIVER PEOPLE

TOR THREW HIS board to the left and missed the snow-crusted brown trunk of a tree. Another branch lashed across his helmet. He flailed his arms, kept his balance by a miracle, and avoided two more trees. A pine tree loomed up, large and ancient. He couldn't possibly avoid it. Then he was past it, and still heading down through the trees. Powder flew up around his board. He skidded around another tree, saw trunks like spears set into the snow, and he knew he was going to fall, when another snowboarder shot in front of him.

"Follow me!" the rider yelled, and Tor realized his coat wasn't blue. This rider was wearing brown and a sweater hung down below the back of the coat. The sweater was a riot of green and purple threads. It was Drake.

Tor felt his board slip into the path carved by Drake

and he concentrated on making sure he stayed there. Behind him he could hear the panting of another rider—Raine? Trees whipped by his head. Most were pine but some were the knotted white of aspen, skeletal in the winter light and reaching for him with bare branches. He knew he couldn't hang on much longer; he was going to fall, and it was going to be terrible. There was a taste like pennies in his mouth.

He didn't fall. He followed Drake's path. The dreadful slope of the mountain wasn't so bad anymore. Drake shot across an open meadow and Tor followed, watching nothing but the flapping edge of Drake's sweater, trying to keep his board upright and going.

Finally, after what seemed like forever, Tor saw that Drake was slowing ahead of him, and Tor was slowing, too. They'd ridden across the dreadful steep side of the mountain and found a gentler slope. Drake came to a stop, and as Tor came up to him, his legs simply gave up and folded under him. He flopped back into the snow.

Tor laid there, his breath coming so fast he couldn't speak, his legs burning with exhaustion, and turned to look at Raine. She was dressed in green and yellow, and her braids hung down the front of her coat like black commas. She sat down in the snow and panted hard. Tor turned his head to Drake. It was the only part of his body he could reliably move. Drake looked as winded as Tor felt.

"Thanks," Tor gasped. Drake was lying flat on his back and his chest heaved. He turned his head to Tor.

"Thank Raine," he said. "Stupid. Following you like that. I had to—had to follow." Drake stopped and panted.

"I couldn't let Tor get killed," Raine said. "I saw you go in here, Tor. I had to—follow you." She stopped to pant some more, too. "What were you doing?"

"I— Max and Jeff were after me," Tor panted.

"Those idiots. They could have gotten you killed," Raine said. "Chasing you around like that, and you're just a beginner."

"Now we're all probably dead," Drake snarled. He was furious.

Tor looked around for the first time and realized that he, Drake, and Raine were sitting at the lip of a steep drop. Before him was a tangled, snow-filled valley covered with aspen, pine, and some kind of tall bush that was spiky and reddish. He could see a creek or a stream very close to them, and as their panting breath started to slow, he could hear the chuckle and gurgle of ice-choked water.

"Where are we?" he asked.

"We're on Borsh Mountain," Drake said. "But I don't know where. I've never been here."

"Neither have I," Raine said in a hushed voice.

"Does anyone come up here?" Tor asked in a whisper. It seemed right to whisper, somehow. The sounds and the noise of Snow Park were completely gone. Tor couldn't even hear the hum of the chairlift machinery. The forest around them was completely deserted and silent. There were no tracks in the snow, either, nothing except their own tracks that led back into the woods and disappeared. They were a long way from the resort. Half a mile? He had no idea how far a snowboard could travel across a mountain, but he knew Drake and Raine had taken a long time to get him under control so they could all stop.

"Nobody," Drake said. He was whispering, too. "This is dangerous. Really dangerous. We're probably all going to die in here. Seriously."

"Why would we die in here?" Tor asked. "The curse?" He didn't say Bigfoot, but he thought it.

"No, silly. Remember, I told you. The mines," Raine whispered back. "This whole mountain is riddled with mines dug by my great-great-great-grandfather. Or so the legend goes. But honestly, Drake, how many mines could one man dig in his lifetime?"

"Enough to kill that hiker back in 1978," Drake said. "Tor, nobody from Snow Park explores this mountain. It's all fenced off wherever there are roads. Back in '78, a hiker went missing. Took a search party a week to find him, and the way they did it was by Mr. Ewald falling into the same mine shaft the hiker had fallen into. Mr. Ewald survived, but he had two broken legs. He landed on the hiker, who was totally dead."

"Mr. Ewald? The math teacher?"

"The very same," Drake said. "Only then he was a teenager helping his dad with the search party. I don't think he was ever the same after he landed on that guy. It took them hours to pull him out."

"Yechh," Tor said.

"I guess there've been other lost people, over the years. The hiker story, that's the only one I know for sure. I heard about one guy they never found. The searchers didn't make it a third of the way up the mountain," Drake said. "They got turned back by aspens so thick you couldn't walk between them, by deadfalls of pines so tall you couldn't get over them, ravines rushing with water, and thickets of raspberry bushes with stickers all over them."

"The mountain doesn't like visitors," Raine said. "That's what my grandma says. I suppose when the mayor takes over the mountain they'll bulldoze down the deadfalls and tear up the aspen trees. They'll fill in the mine shafts, too."

"Unless Bigfoot gets them," Tor said.

"Or he gets us," Drake said.

"We'll be okay, Drake," Raine said. "All we need to do is go downhill, and eventually we'll hit the highway that leads into town. I know we can find that highway."

"Remember that cross-country skier who went missing two years ago? They found him about half a mile from the highway, nearly frozen. But he lived. I guess that's something," Drake said.

"We'll find our way out. Better than Tor going into the White Gates," Raine said.

"The White Gates?" Tor asked.

"You were about half a step from the White Gates," Drake said. "The two chutes that lead down through the trees by the chairlifts. You were about to go into one of them. The other one leads out of bounds, too. They're not double black—they're out of bounds. They're killers."

"I thought the chairlift run looked okay on the map," Tor mumbled, feeling guilty.

"You were trying to go under the chairlifts, and that's just a black. Which you're not ready for anyway. The White Gates are on either side of the chairlift, in the trees, and they're out of bounds, you idiot," Raine said. She put an arm out and smacked Tor on the shoulder. Her mittens were caked with snow. "They're really avalanche chutes and they can't be ridden."

"I was just trying to go under the chairlift part," Tor said. He remembered seeing the White Gates now—the two narrow strips of white that marked the upper part of the mountain. You could see them from the town. They were impossibly high up the mountain and impossibly steep. He felt cold, thinking of ending up in there.

"I know you were trying to get away from Max and

Jeff. Drake and I were waiting to go into the terrain park and we saw you on the chairlift," Raine said.

"What were you thinking, taking that chairlift?" Drake asked.

"I was thinking I could just work my way down slowly," Tor said. "Give them time to get bored and give up."

Drake didn't reply. He put his arms over his head and sighed.

"It would have worked, if you could ride a black diamond run," Raine said, sounding amused. "And if you'd stayed under the chairlifts. Give it at least a couple of weeks before you try that, Tor."

Tor laughed, and Drake snorted, and then everything was all right between them. The trembling in Tor's legs started to go away, and his breath no longer sounded like a dog getting ready to throw up. Drake heaved himself up onto his elbows. Tor copied him and so did Raine, and for a little while they looked over the silent, snow-covered valley. The silence was so intense that Tor found himself hearing things he'd never listened to before: The gurgle of water making its way through ice. A thump of snow falling from a pine tree. The brief chatter of a winter bird, quickly silenced. He felt like holding his breath.

"This valley, why does it look like that?" Tor whispered to Raine. "Those open spaces?"

"That's water. This area looks like it's full of beaver

ponds, and you can see where the river runs through the bottom of the valley," Raine said in a low voice, pointing. "Look at the willow bushes, and those big open spaces, that's water frozen over. And that's—oh!"

She stopped and put a mitten to her mouth. Tor felt Drake stiffen beside him, and then he saw where they were looking.

A dark thing was rising slowly out of the water's edge. It was sleek and brown and looked like an enormous hand.

Bigfoot, thought Tor wildly, and was glad he didn't say it out loud when the hand-looking object finished coming out of the water. It wasn't a hand—it was an entire creature. The animal was about as big as a small dog. It looked exactly like a small, fur-covered human being.

Another one popped out of a hole in the water and the two things ran smoothly up a snow-covered hill. One of them raised up on its haunches and looked around.

"What is that?" Raine said in a whisper so light it sounded like a sigh.

"I don't know," Drake said, his voice just as soft. A third one came pouring out of the hole in the water and glided up the hill.

Then, to their astonishment, the little animals began to slide down the hill. The first one squealed and launched itself into the snow. It slid on its belly until it splashed into the water. The second slid faster than the first, and plunged into the water right after the first. The third jumped into the air and then slid down the same slope, squealing in glee, and shot into the water.

There was silence. The heads popped up again, and they came back out to play.

"They're like people," Raine said softly.

"Like kids," Drake said. Tor could see his face was alight, almost entranced, and he knew his own face must look the same.

"They're not beavers," Raine said.

"Or muskrats," Drake said. "They're way too big for muskrats."

"I know," Tor whispered suddenly. He knew where he'd seen their like—when he visited the San Diego Zoo. "They're otters! These must be river otters!"

"River otters," Raine breathed. "Really?"

"They can't be river otters," Drake whispered flatly.

"Why not?"

"Because there aren't any river otters in Colorado," Drake whispered back. "Not anymore. Aren't they extinct?"

Below them, the otters had finished their game and had disappeared below the surface of the river. Tor could see the path of the snow-covered river in the broad valley that stretched in front of them. A river, and beaver ponds, full of fish and crawdads. No one could reach this place to disturb them. No one knew about them. No one—

"Raine," he said suddenly, turning to her. She looked at him, and saw the knowledge in his face, and realized what he was about to say before he said it.

"The people," she breathed.

"The people. *Her people,*" Drake said from the other side of Tor. Tor turned to see Drake with the same look on his face that Raine had on hers.

"These are Leaping Water's people," Raine said, and her voice was choked. "My great-great-great-grandmother's people. The river people."

"They're real," Drake said. "They're really real."

"Leaping Water wasn't crazy," Tor said. "She really was protecting her people."

"Holy crow," Raine said, and fell back into the snow.

"Well, she *was* crazy," Drake said. "You gotta give her that. But, wow, Raine—look at them!"

Tor watched Raine as she lay in the snow, her helmet and goggles masking everything but her mouth. Her mouth was trembling and tinged slightly blue. He knew he was getting colder by the minute, and there was a terrible empty space in his middle that was telling him that the hamburger he'd had for lunch was far too long ago, and perhaps the way off the mountain would lead them into some dreadful mine shaft and they'd all die. But for just a bit longer he ignored all those thoughts and let the sight of Raine's stunned face and the thought of the otters fill his mind.

This valley was completely undiscovered, another

world right next door to their ordinary lives, and it held creatures that no one knew existed.

"It's like a secret world," Drake murmured, echoing Tor's thoughts exactly. Tor turned to see Drake looking into the valley and grinning in a completely uncomplicated way. This was something, Tor realized, that Drake's famous father had never done. Never seen. Something that no one knew about but them.

"You're right," Tor said, and laughed out loud. He could hear the sound echo through the valley and suddenly a head popped out of the black hole in the water in the valley floor. Tor slapped a hand to his mouth but it was too late. The otter turned its head and looked right at them. The three of them sat and looked at the otter and the otter looked back at them. Tor could see the ink-black shine of its eyes and he held his breath. The otter chirped and then casually turned and sank back under the water.

"He wasn't afraid of us," Drake whispered. "Like he'd never seen humans before."

"He probably hasn't," Tor said.

"We can't tell anyone about this," Raine said.

"Of course not," Tor said immediately. The very idea seemed wrong. This was their magical place. He didn't want to share it with anyone.

A snowflake spiraled out of the air and landed on Raine's helmet. Drake looked up at the sky.

"Snow. We better get back," Drake said. "If we can, that is."

"We can," Raine said, and levered herself to her feet. "I know we can. Can't you feel it now? That the mountain is going to let us go?"

"Yeah," Drake said, "I can." He was grinning but there wasn't the usual edge to it that Tor was used to seeing. Drake looked like a kid, Tor thought. For once, he looked like a kid.

"Me too," Tor said. "Me too."

Raine balanced on her board. She looked worried as a few more snowflakes drifted from the sky.

"Let me lead, Drake. We can't go back the way we came, so we'll all go downhill."

"We can't go back?" Tor asked.

"Uphill all the way, through snow that's hip-deep," Drake said. "We'd never make it."

"We'll snowboard out, Tor. Drake, you follow Tor so if he falls we can stop for him. Okay?" Raine asked.

"Okay," Drake said.

"Okay," Tor said, and ignored the agony of his leg muscles as he got to his feet. His board followed Raine as though it had a mind of its own, and he had one chance to glance back and glimpse the valley where the river people lived before the trees closed in and it was gone.

Tor fell twice and the second time he wasn't sure he could get to his feet. There were thick aspen trees all around him. His board slid out of the path Raine was carving and he caught an edge of a pale white trunk and that was that.

"Come on, Tor, we're almost there," Drake said, holding onto the bole of another aspen tree and looking as calm and rested as if he'd just gotten out of his Sherlock chair. "Listen. Can you hear it?"

Tor held his breath for a moment and he heard a rushing sound like a river. Then he had to breathe, and that was all he heard—his whooping breaths and his pounding heart.

"What was that?" he finally got out.

"The highway," Drake said with a grin. "Raine led us right out. I knew she could. And it's not even dark yet."

Tor used Drake's trick and grabbed the slender bole of an aspen tree. He found his feet and stood, swaying, not knowing if he could force his legs to push his board a foot farther. Then he found himself gliding through the trees and he figured he could, after all.

Raine waited at the edge of the aspens, standing on her board and gazing down into a thick stretch of pines. She was as relaxed on her board as if she was born to it. She grinned at Tor as he slid up to her, showing a stretch of white teeth that shone in what Tor realized was the deepening gloom of late afternoon.

"What time is it?" he asked. His mom was sure to be worried if he didn't show up after the chairlifts closed.

"Four-fifteen," Drake said. "Lift lines just closed. It's

so dark because of the snow that's about to fall. Lots of it, I betcha."

"You're pretty cheerful for a kid who swore we were going to be killed," Raine said, grinning.

"That was before we found your river people," Drake said. "No way I'm going to fall in a mine shaft after seeing them."

"What's that?" Tor said, pointing through the trees. Something large and dark shot by, so fast he couldn't tell what it was. His empty belly tightened in fear. Now what?

"That, my friend, was a semitruck," Raine said, and slapped him on the shoulder. "That's the highway. We're almost home."

The snow started to fall for real as they unstrapped from their snowboards and prepared to climb over the barbed-wire fence that separated them from the highway. Tor noticed with interest the white signs fixed to the wire at intervals: Danger. Private Property. Restricted.

Then they were over. They trudged to the verge of the road and started walking, their boards under their arms. Tor's feet felt odd walking instead of sliding. He was so hungry his stomach growled loudly.

"What was that?" Raine said, looking into the woods. Snow covered her helmet and gathered in her black braids.

"That was me," Tor said. "I'm sorry. I'm really hungry."

Drake started laughing. "You sounded like Bigfoot."

"I could eat a Bigfoot," Tor said. "Seriously."

"We're about a mile from town," Raine said. "When we get there, how about you ask your mom if you can come to our place for dinner? My mom'll feed us all. And we need to talk."

"A powwow?" Drake asked. He'd shoved his goggles up onto his helmet. Tor copied Drake and the day lightened. A little. The snow was swirling down thickly and Tor found himself thinking that the powder was going to be terrific tomorrow. He almost laughed. California seemed very far away.

"A powwow with Ute Girl and Curse Kid, Sweater Boy," Raine said, and a snowball smacked Drake in the shoulder. Raine dusted her free hand on her snowboard. "Left-handed shot, too."

Drake looked ready to scoop out a handful from the snow crusting his board, but suddenly the snow lit up with blue and red light. Tor turned to see a police car right behind them, lights flashing.

"Tor, don't say anything," Raine hissed in his ear. Tor clutched his board tightly under his arm as the police car—actually an enormous SUV with knobby tires—rolled up next to them. Leaning out the window was Coach Rollins, dressed in his Deputy Rollins clothes, and he was frowning.

10 CONNECTIONS

"HELLO, KIDS," DEPUTY Rollins said.

"Hello, sir," Raine and Drake chorused as one. Tor remained silent. They all stopped and stood, their breath smoking in the cold air, the snow falling faster now. The rumble of Deputy Rollins's car blew exhaust toward them and it tasted so bad in his nose and throat that Tor nearly stopped breathing.

"What you doing out here?" Deputy Rollins asked. "Not doing any out-of-bounds riding, are you?"

"No, sir," Drake said. There was a silence, and Tor waited for someone to come up with a reason they were a mile out of town with their snowboards under their arms. Deputy Rollins leaned out the open window and looked at the three of them, his face intent.

"I see. Well, throw your boards in the back and I'll take you into town," he said. "No need to be walking along the highway. It's dangerous out here with a new storm coming in."

Tor looked at Raine and Drake, who shrugged their shoulders a tiny fraction of an inch. What else could they do? They silently stowed their boards in the back of the SUV and climbed into the back. Tor couldn't help heaving a sigh of relief when he sat down. Warm air blew through every vent. He buckled his seat belt and glared at Drake and Raine until they buckled up, too.

"We'll be in town in a minute or two," Deputy Rollins said. Tor, Raine, and Drake sat silently in the back, shoulder to shoulder. Tor looked into the rearview mirror and met Deputy Rollins's interested eyes. He had a look like Tor's old biology teacher, who'd enjoyed dissecting things way too much for Tor's taste.

"Thank you, sir," Tor mumbled.

"I know that Raine's . . . *people* . . . don't particularly care what she does or where she goes, and of course we all know about Drake," Deputy Rollins said. "But I can't imagine that Dr. Sinclair would be happy to find out her son was breaking the law by riding out of bounds. You three were just a few feet from riding into the restricted forest, and that's not just unlawful. You might have been killed."

Drake's shoulder was stiff against Tor's, and Raine's was no better. Tor glanced down to see their hands fisted in their mittens. He looked back up to see Deputy Rollins looking at him again. He opened his mouth and felt two mittens come down on his hands. Raine squeezed on one side, Drake on another. Tor shut his mouth again.

"The snows are too heavy right now for out-of-bounds riding," Deputy Rollins said. The lights of the town were illuminating the swirling snow. Tor saw the neon sign on top of a big gasoline station and knew they were minutes from home. "I might lose some people trying to dig your bodies out from an avalanche. And I'd have to tell your parents. I never enjoy that." The deputy's jaw muscle clenched and Tor believed him. Then his face became smooth again, and he smiled. He met Tor's eyes in the rearview mirror and Tor didn't look away.

"I'd love to see you on the snowboarding team come high school, Tor. But of course you need to choose . . . better companions. We're always looking for fresh blood on the team. If you're still here, that is."

And with that, the deputy pulled up next to the Pro Shop and let them out.

Tor propped his board in the snow and looked at Drake, then at Raine. They were both looking down, their cheeks flushed with anger and perhaps shame. Tor was so hot with fury he wondered if there wasn't actual steam coming from his head. Deputy Rollins drove off, leaving a cloud of choking exhaust behind.

"In San Diego, if the cops don't like you they just shoot you and blame it on the gangs," he said. "This guy's a marshmallow."

Raine's jaw dropped, and so did Drake's as they looked at him. Tor forced his shoulders to shrug. Deputy Rollins had been terrifying, and Tor's suburb of San Diego was peacefully multicultural. But Drake and Raine didn't know that.

Drake sent a plume of white breath out in a choked laugh. "You are *so* in the club," he said.

"Why doesn't he like you?" Tor asked.

"I'm Wexler's son, one step up from a homeless kid living in a Dumpster," Drake said, shrugging. "When I was real little, my dad would sometimes forget about me. He'd leave me in stores or in the park. Once he left me in the car while he was at a bar. It's embarrassing to the cops, to be hauling a little kid in the back of your cop car all the time. And Rollins would never go hassle Todd Wexler about me. He practically worships him."

"You never even tried out for the team," Tor said suddenly. "Did you?"

"Well, I can't try out until I'm in high school, but you're right. I won't try out," Drake said. "And whenever I see Coach Rollins on the mountain I pretend I'm terrible. I fall down, I go real slow. He thinks I'm an idiot."

"Why?" Tor asked.

"You've seen what he turns his riders into," Raine said. "You want to be like them?"

"No way," Tor said instantly.

"And I'm a Ute, grandmother cursed the town, you know the story," Raine said cheerfully. "Let's get some supper. I'm starved. Call your mom from my house?"

"Sure," Tor said. "Uh, where's your house?"

Raine pointed up. Tor looked above the Pro Shop and saw a row of lighted windows.

"We live above our place," she said.

The Douglas home was at the top of a narrow flight of stairs that were reached by a door Tor had never noticed before. The door was right next to the shop and he must have walked past it a dozen times, but he never noticed it until Raine unlocked it with a key and ushered them up the stairs. Tor immediately began to smell something so delicious his stomach woke up again and growled furiously. He was starving.

A light went on at the top of the stairs. Mr. Douglas appeared in the doorway. He looked anxious, and then he gave a big sigh.

"I was starting to get worried," he said. "Drake, good to see you. Er, Tor?"

"Yes, sir," Tor said, feeling awkward.

"We're inviting him for dinner, is that okay, Dad?" Raine said in a rush. "Can we get out of our clothes and wipe down our boards? We're starving and Tor has to call his mom—"

"Enough, enough," Mr. Douglas said, laughing and stepping back. "Get in here and strip down. I'll get the phone."

Tor followed Raine and Drake into a large room filled with shelves, pegs for snowboards, benches to sit on, and places for wet snow boots. It was warm and dry, and the smell of whatever was cooking in the Douglas apartment smelled even better in here, if that was possible.

Tor called his mom, who sounded pleased that he had an invitation to dinner. He turned to Raine. "She said okay."

"Great," Raine said.

"If I don't eat soon, I'm going to start eating my sweater," Drake said.

Drake's sweater was patterned with watermelon and lime slices on an orange background. The sweater might have been brightly colored when it was new, but the colors had faded to shades that defied description, as though the fruit wasn't exactly from planet Earth. Tor nodded in approval. This had to be the worst sweater yet.

Dinner was a crowded affair, because Raine's family included her parents, her younger brother, Carswell, and a grandmother so ancient and wrinkled she looked like a mummy Tor had once seen on the cover of a nature magazine. Her eyes were as sparkling as pools of black oil set in her seamed face, and she took a great interest in Tor. She held his hand and examined his palm, pinched his cheek like she was testing fresh bread at the store, and touched his hair with her gnarled fingers.

"You're starving," she announced, after stepping away from him, and Raine's family laughed as one.

"I could have told you that," Raine said. "Let's eat!"

Tor had finished a second bowl of a savory stew, scooping it up with a thick tortilla they called fry bread, before he could think of anything but the need of filling the enormous hole in his belly. When he looked up, he met the black eyes of Grandma Douglas, looking at him like he was the most fascinating thing she'd ever seen. She winked at him. He smiled back at her, as fascinated by her as she was by him. This was the great-granddaughter of Leaping Water. Had she been there when Leaping Water cursed the town?

"I was there," Grandma Douglas said, reading Tor's mind as easily as though he'd spoken. "But I was only seven. I was in school and missed the whole thing, darn it."

Mr. Douglas jumped in surprise and Mrs. Douglas dropped a piece of fry bread into her stew. Mrs. Douglas was a delicate little woman with short-cut black hair and a heart-shaped face. She made a little "o" sound of distress.

"You heard about it, though?" Tor asked, ignoring Raine's parents.

"My whole life," Grandma Douglas said. "My

husband never cared about the legends, though. Short though it was, his life."

"Vietnam," Raine mouthed across the table.

"He was a navigator on B-52's," Grandma Douglas said proudly. "Carswell Douglas, one of the great-grandsons of Chief Douglas of the Ouray Utes. We met at a dance on the reservation in Utah. I found a job as a teacher there after I graduated from college. I wanted to know my roots, and there was Carswell at the door of the Corn Festival dance, all six foot of him, all the roots I ever wanted."

Grandma Douglas sighed like a girl. Raine looked fondly at her grandma.

"When my husband died in the war, I came back to Snow Park and worked in the store for my parents. I had Merrill by then, though he was just a baby. Merrill has a hawk's eyes, do you see? So many hours in the air, my husband, he gave his son those eyes."

"Oh, Mom," Mr. Douglas said, with his fierce hawk's eyes blinking out of his face. Raine gave a happy little giggle.

"Well, they do look like a bird's eyes," she said. "Don't you think, Tor?"

"Yeah," Tor said. "They really do."

"These young ones have things to do," Grandma announced, shoving back her chair and using her hands to lift herself to her feet. She was so tiny she hardly looked taller standing up. "We'll do the dishes, Raine. You three can have the study."

As Raine showed them toward the study and her parents started the dishes with bemused looks on their faces, Grandma Douglas took Tor's arm in a grip that felt like lobster pinchers.

"It's about time you showed up," she whispered, and winked at him in a way that left him as bewildered as Raine's parents.

The study contained shelf after shelf of books, surrounding an enormous library desk that held open books, papers, and a computer. The drapes were drawn, but Tor could see that in daylight the sun would shine in from Main Street and paint big squares of sunshine on the worn rug and the comfortable reading chairs.

"It's our place," Raine said, eyeing the old carpet and the threadbare drapes as though seeing them for the first time. She sounded a little ashamed.

"This is the best place ever," Tor said. "All those windows, right over the street. Hey, you have an Internet connection? We can find out about the otters!"

"Shhh," Raine said. "Not so loud, they'll hear you." Still, she looked pleased. Drake, who'd been silent until now, stretched his arms out and yawned.

"They won't hear us with the door closed," he said. "This is where I sleep when I stay here."

Tor looked over and saw an old couch filled with comfy, tasseled pillows. He suddenly yawned so widely his jaw creaked. He wanted nothing more than to flop down on all that softness and go to sleep.

"Raine, what about the mining claim?" Drake asked suddenly.

"What?" Raine said.

"The mining claim," Tor said. He clenched his fists. "Isn't the mining claim going to be . . . whats-its?"

"Disinherited," Raine said. Her mouth thinned down to a slash. "That's right. They're going to bulldoze the mountain and turn it into another slope for the resort."

"No, they *can't*," Drake said. He put a hand to his forehead like he'd been struck. "The otters."

"They're not going to take away their home. They just can't," Tor said.

"If they're an endangered species, won't that mean that Mayor Malone will have to stop?" Drake said.

"Let's find out," Raine said, and sat down at the computer.

Ten minutes later, they had their answer.

" 'River otters were once widely distributed in riparian habitats statewide, but free-range populations were extirpated from Colorado early in the twentieth century,' " Raine read out loud.

"Riparian?" Drake asked.

"Rivers," Raine said.

"Extirpated?" Tor asked.

"Let me guess," Drake said. "That's a nice way of saying exterminated."

"Yeah," Raine said. "Turned into hats and gloves for rich ladies. Now hush and let me go on. 'In 1975 the river otter was designated as a state endangered species. The Colorado Division of Wildlife reintroduced one hundred twenty-two river otters into five separate locations in 1976. River otters were downlisted to threatened in 2003.'" Raine sighed and sat back from the computer. Tor craned forward to take a look. A picture of a river otter was on her screen. It had ink-black eyes that looked just like Grandma Douglas.

"That's it, then," Drake said. "We reveal them, the bulldozers have to stop. They're endangered, right?"

"Threatened," Raine corrected. "I think that makes all the difference in the world. Threatened. So we tell everyone, and the Division of Wildlife puts out traps and moves them somewhere else, and the bulldozers start up."

Tor felt like gagging. The thought of the otters caught and caged was too horrible to think about, but he was already thinking about it. They'd cry. He didn't know how he knew that, but he did. They'd cry in their metal cages, and they'd die on a strange river far away from their home. And that would be okay because they were only threatened, not endangered. No one would care.

"Now we know why Leaping Water cursed the town," he said. "We have to save them."

"If we can save them, Tor," Raine said slowly, "would that mean the curse would be broken?"

"The healer has to promise to protect the people," Drake said. "But if the healer's son protects them, wouldn't that do it?"

"I don't know," Tor said, but he felt hope light up inside him like a warm flame.

"It's worth a try," Drake said. "I'd say, worth a try."

"Time to go, Tor," Mr. Douglas said from the doorway. "It's a school night."

The next day Tor dropped by the Snow Park Medical Clinic after his snowboard lesson, his board caked with powder and his belly growling for supper. He heard his mother's voice in her office.

"Tor doesn't know," Dr. Sinclair said. Tor froze.

He was planning to eat supper, work on homework, do research on otters and mining claims and National Forest legal issues, and finally get some sleep before it started all over again. Tor had never been so busy in his life. He'd also never been happier. Now he stood very still, listening, because his mom was on the phone and she was talking about him.

"No, I'm not bringing him to Detroit, Shareena," Dr. Sinclair said, and barked out a choked laugh. "I'd love for you to meet him, he's just the best kid you've ever met. . . . What? . . . No, it isn't the weather, or the crime. It's that I'd never be home, I'd always be at the hospital. . . .

Yes? . . . No, even if you made him a whole necklace of *gris-gris* with every voodoo protection . . . What?"

This time Dr. Sinclair laughed louder. Tor could smell the tea his mother favored, a pungent brew mixed with warm milk that she called Chai. She'd gotten a taste for it from her Indian friend, a nurse called Sarah—Sarah from India. Tor gripped his snowboard with his mittens, hoping he wouldn't betray his presence in the hall. His mom had gone away and made voodoo friends like Shareena, who wanted to give him *gris-gris*, whatever that meant. She had an Indian friend who wore a red dot on her forehead and drank tea that smelled like Tor imagined India itself must smell—rich and full of incense, like the fur of a tiger. He didn't want his mother to go back to those people and that exotic life and send him away.

"No, you can't do that to Stanford Malone, girlfriend. That would be against your rules, now wouldn't it? . . . Yeah, I guess so. I don't think he wants me because of my deathless beauty or anything, for heaven's sake. I mean, you know what I look like."

You're very pretty! Tor thought fiercely.

"There's something else, besides me not wanting to date the mayor. Like the town doesn't want me here. I'm failing here and I don't know why and I can't stop it and I'm so angry I could . . . oh, look at the time, I've got to go."

The curse, Tor thought. It's the stupid curse.

He crept backward a few steps and then clumped

147

loudly up and down in the hall. Dr. Sinclair poked her head out of her office door and her face lit up with a smile at the sight of him.

"Hi, Tor," she said. "Shrimp etoufee tonight, sound good?"

"Sounds great," he said. "I'm going to study at Raine's afterward, that all right?"

"Sure. Let me get my stuff," his mom said, and ducked back into her office. There was something he could do about the curse, Tor realized as he waited for his mom. There was something he could try.

Mayor Malone was at the center of everything. His ancestor, Dr. Robert Malone, had tried to take over Leaping Water's mountain. Now Mayor Malone was trying to take it, this time by disinheriting the mining claim. The curse that Leaping Water had laid on the town was supposed to protect her river people, but now they were in more danger than ever.

Unless Tor could find the original mining claim, the bulldozers would be ripping out trees by next summer, the otters would be gone, and he and his mother would never escape the curse.

He *had* to figure out what was going on, and he had to do it soon.

Drake was at Raine's apartment when Tor arrived. Drake's father was in Chile doing a snowboarding video with the famous Warren Miller, a name that Tor didn't know but as a snowboarder he was obviously supposed to practically worship. Drake was at Raine's for a week or so, an arrangement that seemed to be no big deal to anyone.

"What're you doing here?" Drake asked as Raine opened the door. The apartment was quiet—Grandma Douglas had already retired to bed and Raine's parents had gone to a movie with her little brother. The apartment was theirs.

"I need your help," Tor said shortly. "That's what I'm doing here." Then he explained what he meant to do. Alone or with them, he meant to go ahead with his plan.

"That's crazy," Drake said when Tor finished. He turned and started rummaging in a duffel bag that sat by the couch in the study where he slept. Raine stood motionless, her only movement the glitter of her dark eyes looking from Drake to Tor.

"Well, we can't go to prison, right?" she finally asked.

"No way," Tor said. "We're kids. Maybe probation."

"Our reputations will be in tatters," Drake said. "How will we deal with the shame?" He pulled off his sweater, a woolen thing that had been stitched together from triangles of loudly contrasting colors, and held up a fleece jersey that was plain, midnight black. "All right, then. Let's go break into the mayor's office."

11 ☠ CHEATERS

BREAKING INTO THE mayor's office proved easier than it sounded, since Raine had a key.

"Skeleton key," she explained, rummaging in a kitchen drawer that held screwdrivers, sewing thread, three pairs of pliers, and what looked like an antique doorknob. Raine finally made a satisfied sound and held up an enormous piece of metal that looked like something from a horror movie. It was brownish-black, as long as Raine's hand, and the keys were like big square teeth. "The mayor's office is in the same row of buildings as ours."

"You have the keys to the whole building?" Tor asked. Raine had changed into black jeans and a tight black top that zipped to her neck. With her black hair in her usual long braids she looked like a junior ninja. A Ute ninja.

"That's a key?" Drake said, taking the key from Raine. "It looks like a joke."

"The front door locks have been changed a million times," Raine said, snatching the key back and tucking it into a little bag she slung from her shoulder. "But not the alley doors, where the trash gets taken out. They're all the same locks. Ours too. Don't tell anyone."

"Never," Drake said, looking delighted. "Of course. Flashlights?"

"Look in that drawer," Raine commanded, and Tor rummaged in another kitchen drawer that held more tools, a cake slicer that looked like an enormous comb, three napkin rings shaped like turkeys, and two flashlights.

"What time does the movie get out?" Tor asked.

"They'll be home by nine-thirty," Raine said. "To get Carswell to bed."

"Then we don't have a lot of time," Tor said. He clicked the flashlight on and off. "You sure about this?"

Drake made a disdainful sound and didn't answer.

"Too bad we don't have tranquilizer darts," Raine said, shoving her flashlight into her little bag and heading for the apartment door.

"Why?" Tor asked.

"Because if we find the mining claim there, you'll need to shoot me with one," Raine said. "Before I find the mayor." She bared her teeth and looked at Tor with her glittering black eyes. He remembered how her ancestors had killed Nathan Meeker because they didn't want to learn how to farm, and he tried not to grin, but he had to anyway. He was really glad she was on his side.

The alley was dark and grimy. The snow had been tramped over until it was the consistency and color of oatmeal flakes. Their boots slipped on the dirty snow, but at least they left no tracks. The alley was filled with Dumpsters, some tall and some round. The other side of the alley was a long brick wall. Tor found time to marvel that there wasn't a single piece of graffiti on the entire wall. Two dim sodium lights lit the alleyway at either end, making eerie shadows that were ink black or grayish-orange.

Tor could hear Snow Park's Main Street but it sounded distant and muffled. There was the rumble of traffic, the occasional squeal or shout of someone hailing someone else, and a deep pounding beat of music from a bar on Main Street. Raine led them silently down the alley and stopped once, in the black shadow of a large Dumpster, while a car cruised slowly past the side entrance to the alley.

Then the car was past, and Raine walked on as silently as a ghost. They had nearly reached the end of the alley when she turned to a doorway and pulled her big key out of her bag. They were all wearing gloves.

They'd all seen enough television shows to know about fingerprints and DNA. Besides, it was cold.

The door creaked open slowly and Raine walked in, her shoulders tense and hunched. Drake slid in after her with an ease that reminded Tor of the otters pouring out of their hole in the river, and then he, too, was inside and Raine was shutting the door behind them.

"So far, so good," Drake whispered. "Flashlights?"

"Let me check the blinds first," Raine whispered. She squeezed her fingers over the lens and then clicked on her flashlight so it cast a faint, reddish glow. Tor could see the room they were standing in, lit by Raine's dim light. There were two big plastic tubs overflowing with papers, a copy machine that looked expensive but whose paper door was broken and hanging half-off, a small steel box half-buried behind boxes of paper, and a big garbage can that smelled like old coffee grounds and cold French fries. They were in a storage room.

Raine opened another door gently and eased through it. A moment later she was back, and her flashlight was unhooded.

"The blinds are pulled down," she said. "Try not to shine your light around too much, anyway."

Tor could feel a shivering ache deep inside him. He'd never done anything like this before, and he felt guilty and ashamed. But he was also desperate.

They might save the otters. They might save Raine's

family land from the bulldozers of the developers. They might break the curse that was on his mom and also on him, or find out who was using the *idea* of the curse to blame his mom for Brian Slader's death.

Or were all these things somehow intertwined, like the pipes and wires under the streets? Tor stood for a moment, lost in thought, trying to follow the threads down to a connection point. Was there a connection there? He felt there was, but what?

"Let's go," Drake hissed, and whatever had been hovering in Tor's mind was gone. He blinked and reached for his flashlight.

The mayor's office was handsome, neat as a pin, and empty of papers of any kind except for the certificates and photos hung on the wall. Drake made a snorting sound when he saw the photos of the mayor next to one of the more famous Denver Broncos quarterbacks.

"He should have a picture with a snowboarder," he said, and Tor could hear a touch of reluctant pride in his voice. "We've got world-class snowboarders here. Who cares about football in Snow Park?"

"Everybody," Raine said absently, looking at the contents of the mayor's desk. "Everybody watches football, Drake. Sometimes even when there's a powder day."

Tor snorted at the same time as Drake, and they shared a grin across the beams of their flashlights.

"There's nothing here," Raine announced. "We need

to look in the back room, where all that paper is. Or maybe there's a filing room we missed?"

Tor gently opened doors until he found what looked like a break room. There were filing cabinets in there and he hissed at the others to join him. A coffee machine sat next to a sink where coffee cups were placed, clean and upside down, on a paper towel. There was a refrigerator in the room and Drake opened it and yelped in surprise when the interior light came on, dazzling as the sun after their dim flashlights, showing a fridge with soda pop, coffee creamers, and some left-behind lunch items.

Tor blinked after Drake closed the door, because he saw nothing but a purple afterimage of the lightbulb in the darkness, but also because there was something important about the fridge. What was it?

"Hey," he said. "There was a fridge-looking thing in the back room, too. Did you see it? It was shoved way in the back, but it was there. It looks like one of the fridges in my mom's clinic."

"I didn't see it," said Drake, rubbing his eyes. Raine was already going through the files but with a droop to her shoulders that meant she'd nearly given up.

"There was. At the back of the room, by the trash containers. Why was it there? Nobody needs two fridges, do they?"

"Let's go look," Raine said. "But why would anyone store a mining certificate in a fridge?"

"They might not store certificates," Tor said. "But they might store drugs."

The fridge was a box made of polished steel and it was hidden behind the broken-down copy machine and a big box of paper trash.

"Doesn't look like a fridge," Raine said. They all pointed their flashlights at it.

"Let's see," Tor said, and he crouched down. He had to push a box of papers out of the way to open the door, and he could feel the excitement making his fingers tremble and the flashlight beam jitter. This was a hidden thing, and it was important.

The door came open, and Tor took a little hop back and sat down. The flashlights wavered wildly in Raine's and Drake's hands, and Tor had to hold his flashlight in both hands so he could aim it at the contents of the humming refrigerator.

It was full of blood.

It left no footprints in the snow and it left no cloud-breath of air behind it. Dr. Sinclair dropped her medical bag in the snow and stepped back. The creature was right in front of her. The face was pale and remote as snow crystals, and the blood that rimmed its mouth was as red and damp as a fresh rose petal. As it reached for her, Dr. Sinclair began to scream.

* * *

Tor remembered his forgotten dream with complete clarity, like he was living it all over again.

"Vampires," he breathed.

"Is that blood?" Raine said in a squeaky little voice.

"That's blood," Drake said. "Isn't it, Tor?"

"It's blood," Tor said. There was no mistaking the blood bags, hung from the top of the fridge by hooks and swaying slightly. Tor had seen blood bags before because his dad always donated blood to the Red Cross. His dad had taken him along so he wouldn't be afraid of donating someday when he was a grown-up, too.

"You think we got vampires in this town?" Drake asked.

"The mayor is a *vampire*?" Raine said.

Tor remembered how the mayor was trying to kiss his mom, and he was glad he was sitting down because he felt all the strength drain out of him all over again. Was the mayor trying to—?

"Ewww," he said. He felt like throwing up.

"Wait a minute," Drake said, leaning in. "There are labels on those bags—one of them says Malone."

"Stanford Malone?" Raine asked, "Mayor Malone?"

"No," Drake said. "*Jeff* Malone."

There was such complete silence in the room that the humming sound of the fridge sounded huge and loud, like a jet engine revving for takeoff.

"That's *Jeff Malone's* blood?" Raine asked from above

Tor's head, where he still sat and pointed his flashlight at the swaying blood bags and thought hard. There were other bags, too. One was marked "Max Nye," and another one was marked "Brian Slader."

Brian Slader. The boy who died.

"Wait a minute—" he started to say, but then a noise interrupted him. There was a loud clicking sound and then the rumble of street traffic. At the front of the office, someone had just opened the outside door.

Tor's heart felt like he'd just been kicked in the chest. He shut the fridge door and it sucked closed with a horrible sound, too loudly, but Drake was already opening the back door to the alley and there was no time to do anything but run. Tor covered his flashlight instead of clicking it off and followed Raine, who was already crowding Drake out the door.

The alley seemed as light as noon after the dimness of the mayor's office. Raine locked the door with her huge skeleton key, fingers shaking so badly the key chattered around the old lock before sliding in. She turned it, withdrew it, and they ran down the alley as fast as they could, their pounding feet muffled by the grimy snow.

Raine threw the back door of the Pro Shop open and skidded in. Drake followed and Tor jumped in behind him. Raine turned and locked the door with her ancient key.

"The front, quick!" she hissed. Tor followed her

and Drake through the darkened shop toward the front windows.

Outside was the worst thing Tor could think of—the flashing blue and red lights of Deputy Rollins's big SUV. It was pulled up in front of the mayor's office and they watched, invisible and still as mannequins behind the window display of coats and skis, as the deputy left the mayor's office and looked suspiciously up and down the street.

As soon as he turned away, Raine pulled Tor and Drake back from the window.

"We need to get back upstairs, quick," Drake whispered.

"This way," Raine said. "There's a back set of stairs."

When the apartment door opened ten minutes later, Raine leaned out casually from the study.

"Hi, Mom," she said. "Hi, Dad. How was the movie?"

Tor was behind the computer screen typing furiously, his ears stinging from the toweling he'd given his hair to get it dry. Drake was back in his sweater of the many awful triangles, sprawled like a cat in the corner of his sofa, and Raine was dressed in gray sweatpants and a fluffy jersey with an imprint of an owl on the pocket. Her ninja look was gone.

"Hi, kids," Mr. Douglas said. "I'll go check the shop," he told his wife, and kissed her on the cheek. Carswell was in her arms, a little bundle of eight-year-old boy asleep with his head on his mother's shoulder. Mr. Douglas kissed his son's head. "Back in a minute."

"What's up?" Raine asked.

"Deputy Rollins said someone reported an attempt at a break-in tonight," Mrs. Douglas said, frowning. "Lights in the mayor's office, or next door at Taffy's Candle Shop. The person wasn't sure. At any rate, I'm sure it was just reflections or something. Let me get this boy to bed, he weighs a ton."

"Okay," Raine said. When Mrs. Douglas came out of Carswell's bedroom she was frowning at her watch.

"You need to get home, Tor, don't you?" Mrs. Douglas said. "It's nearly nine-thirty."

Tor jumped to his feet. He'd completely forgotten about his own curfew, which was nine.

"Oh, man, I gotta go," he said.

"I'll call your mom," Mrs. Douglas said. Her face was kind. "I'll tell her you forgot the time. You just get your coat and you'll be home while I'm still talking to her."

Tor threw a glance of frustration at Raine and Drake, who looked at each other and then at him. There had been no time to talk, no time to work things out.

"Do you want me to walk you home?" Drake said suddenly.

"It's only a block, dear," Mrs. Douglas said absently, pecking out Tor's number on her phone.

Drake looked intently at Tor, who felt a cold chill

down his spine. It was nighttime, and he would be alone. In the darkness.

"I'll run," he said.

"Run fast," Drake said.

"Nothing makes sense," Raine said at lunch the next day. She wore interesting loops in her braids, round shells with turquoise beads at the end of leather fringe. The braid decorations seemed very Ute to Tor. This was the first time he'd seen Raine wear anything remotely, well, Indian.

None of them was eating very much. The meal was spaghetti, and the sauce was too thin and runny for Tor to stomach. It looked too much like blood. The lunchroom was roaring, a sound so frantic and fueled with holiday spirits they could have shouted across the table at each other and no one would have paid a bit of attention.

"I know it doesn't," Tor said. "But somehow it all fits. We can't see the connection, but it's there."

"They can't be vampires," Drake said. "In the movies it's the good vampires who store blood in their fridge. Right? Good vampires drink from blood banks, bad vampires kill their victims. Isn't that the way it works?" He was wearing what Tor thought of as his Bigfoot sweater today, the one with lots of colors and tufts of yarn poking out and hanging down.

"I think so," Raine said doubtfully. "I haven't watched many vampire shows."

"I have," Drake and Tor chorused as one.

"So Mayor Malone has his kid's blood supply in a fridge," Tor said. "We rule out vampires because, well—"

"People would be dropping like flies all over town," Drake said confidently, and Tor nodded. "And turning into vampires, too. That's what happens in the books and movies."

"So no vampires," Raine said. "So the mayor is hiding the snowboarding team's blood. What on earth can you do with blood? What could they use it for? Tor, are you okay?"

Tor had dropped his head into his hands. He knew, just like that. He'd figured it out. He raised his face to Drake and Raine, who were looking at him anxiously. Drake saw his expression and his eyes lit up.

"You know!" Drake said. "What is it?"

"*Bicycle racing*," Tor said. "I heard about this because of bicycle racing. My dad, he follows the Tour de France, that's a big bike race, they ride across France and—"

"And you're babbling," Raine said sharply. "What is it?"

"Blood doping," Tor said. "The snowboarding team is blood doping."

Drake sat back, his jaw dropping. Raine just looked more puzzled.

"Of course," Drake said furiously. "Of course. The whole snowboarding team was in on it. They were blood doping!"

"Blood doping?" Raine said. "What's that?"

"You take your own blood out of your body and store it," Tor said. "As though you're donating blood, except you keep it instead. Your body replaces the lost blood over a month or so. Then right before you race, you use a machine called a centrifuge to strip out the red blood cells and you inject those back into your body. For a day or so, until your body absorbs the extra red blood cells, you have a big edge. Extra red blood cells mean you can carry more oxygen, your muscles work better, and you can race faster."

"And it's undetectable," Raine said. "Of course! It's not a drug. It's your *own blood.*"

"Mayor Malone is blood doping the snowboarding team before competitions," Drake said. "He's cheating."

"It's like they're drinking their own blood," Raine said, looking revolted. "That's disgusting."

"We have to tell someone," Drake said.

"Of course we do," Tor said. "But who's going to believe us?"

"Not Sheriff Hartman," Drake said. "He's tight with Deputy Rollins. And you know what Rollins would say about this."

"He'd never believe us," Raine said, and stabbed her fork into her mess of untouched spaghetti. "He thinks we're wasters. He knows Jeff Malone hates you and he'd just think we were trying to get back at him."

"Yeah, I think you're right," Tor said. "We can't go to the mayor, obviously. He's the bad guy we're trying to catch. Not the town doctor, she's in as much trouble as we are." He smiled at the two of them, but it was a smile that hurt.

Raine let her fork go and gripped her hands together. "Not the town doctor, no," she said, and Tor wondered for a bleak moment if next year Raine would be here with Drake, just the two of them eating lunch together, and "Dr. Susan Sinclair" would have been added to her list of doctors affected by the curse. And Tor, where would he be? What lunchroom would he be sitting in? He squeezed his eyes shut at the wave of desolation that threatened to roll over him.

"I know," he said. The answer had come to him. "I know who to tell."

12 ☠ PURSUIT

"WELL, TOR, DRAKE, Raine," Ms. Adams said, as the class filed out through the double doors. "What's up?" She was dressed in purple today, purple velvet jeans and an enormous purple sweater.

"Can we talk to you?" Raine asked. "Alone?"

"Of course," Ms. Adams said, looking confused. She pointed with her wand toward her office, a cramped and mostly unused room. She raised an eyebrow. "In here, then, if you want privacy."

Ms. Adams's eyebrows, as red as her hair, climbed even higher when Drake shut the door, closing them into the small little office. She sat down without a word and faced them.

"We need to ask you some things," Tor said, after Raine and Drake looked over at him. This was his idea, and he had to start. He swallowed because his mouth seemed to be terribly dry all of a sudden.

"Anything," Ms. Adams said, and she laid down her wand, which was gripped rather tight in her hands. She held her palms out to them. "This is just me. Ask me."

"Okay," Tor said. "Here's the thing. What would you do—what would you say—if you found a bunch of blood?"

"Blood?" Ms. Adams said. She picked up her wand and gripped it. Her freckles stood out clearly on her face and Tor realized she'd gone white. "Where?"

"Stored in bags," Drake said. "Hidden away in a fridge. Blood. Human blood."

"Not at my mom's clinic," Tor said. This wasn't going right at all. Ms. Adams looked completely confused. "Stored away in secret."

"Where?" she asked.

"We can't tell you," Raine said.

"But we don't know what it means," Tor said. "At first we thought, well, we thought it might be—"

"Vampires," Ms. Adams said immediately, and laughed out loud. "Don't look so surprised, you three. I've read lots of vampire fiction. If I saw a hidden fridge full of fresh human blood, that's the first thing I'd think."

"But we figured it couldn't be, not in the real world," Raine said faintly.

Ms. Adams twirled her wand absently in her fingers.

Tor was so amazed by Ms. Adams saying the word "vampire" that he expected to see sparks shoot out the end, or maybe a frog, as though she was a real elf and she had a real magic wand.

"The world is full of more amazing things than you know," Ms. Adams said. "Don't come to me if you want reassurance that the world is solid." She looked at them, her blue eyes as clear and cool as water, and Tor felt like the world had a trapdoor and he was sitting on top of it and it was about to open.

"One of the names on the bags was Jeff Malone," Drake said. "Jeff hates Tor. He ran him out of bounds and about killed him. Then we see this name on the bag in the ma—in the place where the blood was."

"Jeff's having a hard time right now," Ms. Adams said. "Brian Slader died and he's grieving about that. Dr. Sinclair took care of Brian, so Jeff wants to lash out at Tor. It's a natural thing for him to do, although it's not the *right* thing."

Tor suddenly sat bolt upright. He could feel his heart thudding and it was getting louder and louder in his chest until he thought everyone could hear it. Drake didn't see. He continued with Ms. Adams.

"We think maybe Jeff isn't so angry at Tor as he is about a doctor being in town," Drake continued. "A doctor who could figure out what the snowboarding team is doing."

"What are they doing?" Ms. Adams asked.

"Blood doping," Raine said. "We think they're blood doping. Have you heard of it?"

"I have," Ms. Adams said. "This is a very serious charge, you know."

"It's more serious than you realize," Tor said slowly. His heart thudded even louder now. All the final connections were falling into place.

"It's cheating, that's what it is," Drake said. "Cheaters. Dirty *cheaters.*"

"It's more than cheating," Tor said, feeling breathless. "The first night I was here, Brian Slader took sick with pumo—polo—edema something."

"Pulmonary edema," Ms. Adams said gently. "High-altitude sickness where the lungs fill with fluid."

"He didn't die of that," Tor said. "My mom told me. He got edema because he was low on blood. He died of *blood loss.*"

There was a thunderstruck silence in the room and then there was a tiny, echoing snap. Ms. Adams looked dazedly down at her hands. She'd broken her wand in two.

"They took too much blood," Raine said. She put her hands over her face and burst into tears. "They took too much blood."

"They didn't mean to," Drake said, patting her shoulder awkwardly. "Don't cry, Raine."

"It's the curse, I know it," she wept.

"No!" Tor shouted. He was standing but he didn't

remember getting to his feet. "That's not it at all! The mayor is using the curse, don't you see? When Brian got sick, and then died, he had the perfect person to blame it on. The town doctor. My mom. Because of the curse."

"You're right, Tor," Raine said. She lifted her face from her hands. Tears still marked her cheeks but she looked furiously angry. "He's been using my great-great-great-grandmother's curse to blame Tor's mom for Brian's death and all along it was *his fault.*"

"What is important," Ms. Adams said, "is who is doing this? And why are you sure it's the mayor?" She took the pieces of her wand and dropped them one by one into the trash. The can was empty and the wood rattled hollowly as it struck the bottom. She opened her desk drawer and took out a thin case. It was made of worn black leather. Ms. Adams opened it and took out another director's baton. It was highly polished and had a reddish gleam.

"It's got to be Mayor Malone," Tor said, his eyes on the wand. It looked very old.

"Mayor Malone," Raine said.

"The mayor," Drake said. "Who else could it be?"

"This was my grandfather's," Ms. Adams said, letting her fingers smooth over the wand. "I don't use it often, but since I seem to have destroyed my director's baton, well . . ."

"What do we do?" Raine asked. Ms. Adams nodded, her hands still smoothing the wand. Tor knew suddenly that she was using her grandfather's memory, her grandfather's strength, to help her. The job of a choir director didn't usually involve solving a murder, Tor thought, and bit his lip to keep back a shaky laugh. He was suddenly very glad that they'd chosen to talk to Ms. Adams.

"You came to me," she said. "I don't feel much like a brave and powerful adult, to tell you the truth. You gave me a puzzle with all the pieces put together. But I can't wave my baton and make everything better." She waved it, in demonstration.

"You can't go to the sheriff," Raine said.

"He won't believe you," Drake said. "He wouldn't believe us."

"Nor can I go to the mayor, or the city council," Ms. Adams continued. "I'm new here, too, remember. I don't know if the mayor is involved or not—"

Drake, Raine, and Tor all opened their mouths as one, but Ms. Adams held up a hand. "But nevertheless, I have an idea who might be able to help us."

Tor felt warm clear through when Ms. Adams said "us."

"The FBI?" Drake asked.

"The governor?" Raine asked.

"The CBI," Ms. Adams said. "Colorado Bureau of Investigation. My husband has a friend who knows an agent who works there. It's a lousy connection, a friend-of-a-friend sort of thing, but I might be able to use it. Listen to me, though. You can't talk to anyone about this. Anyone. Is that clear?" She looked sternly at them.

Tor, Drake, and Raine exchanged amused glances.

"You think?" Drake said.

Ms. Adams made a half-choked laughing sound. "Of course," she said. "You've kept this secret quite well so far, haven't you? Can you take the CBI officer, if I can get one up here, to the blood?"

"Yes," Drake said.

"Fingerprints would help, on the fridge," Ms. Adams continued. "Not yours."

"We wore gloves," Raine said.

"That's good. I don't know if it'll be enough, but it's a start. Just keep your heads down for a day or so and let me do my grown-up thing, all right?"

"Deal," Tor said, and felt relief wash over him like warm water.

"Okay," Drake said, and frowned. He didn't look very relieved.

"Yes," Raine said. She looked hopeful.

"Now go on," Ms. Adams said. "I'll clear up a few last things and I'll head home to work on this. Best if we're not seen leaving the building together, not right now."

That was something Tor hadn't thought about. Were they being watched? He looked around as the three of them walked down the empty corridors and out of the school, but there wasn't anyone around. No Mayor

Malone in his expensive tan coat, no blue coats, no stick-figure vampires in the glare of the snowy afternoon.

"Let's go snowboarding," Drake suggested, as they crunched across the street. "Why not? We have to stay out of sight, right? We'll hang with you on the easy slopes, Tor, so Jeff and Max'll leave you alone. Want to, Raine?"

"I'd love to," Raine sighed. "I can't believe it about—"

"Shhh," Tor said. "No talking about it. Drake's right. Let's ride."

A few minutes later Tor was stripping out of his school clothes. Raine's flashlight from their trip to the mayor's office was sitting on his dresser. He reminded himself to give it back to her and zipped it into a deep pocket of his snowboarding pants. He shoved some granola bars in various other pockets and then headed down to the clinic to see his mom. He didn't really have a reason to see her, except he wanted to see her. He wasn't going to tell her anything, of course. He wasn't going to tell her that they'd solved the mystery of Brian Slader's death and were going to stop the mayor and break the curse.

He kept telling himself that as he walked up the clinic steps, nearly bouncing in his excitement. Everything was going to be solved. Some CBI guy would drive into town like an action hero and arrest the bad guys, and Mayor Malone would go to jail, and Raine's mountain would stay untouched for the otters, and he and his mom would stay here in Snow Park.

Tor set his snowboard on the porch and opened the door to the clinic, happiness bubbling inside him. Even the sight of Mrs. Colm couldn't destroy his good feeling. He grinned at Mrs. Colm too widely and she glared at him suspiciously.

"Is my mom in?" he asked.

"She's with a patient," Mrs. Colm said coldly.

"I'll just leave her a note," Tor said, and walked down the hall to his mother's office. He passed the first patient room, empty and quiet, and realized the room didn't have a refrigerator in it like the other rooms did. There was an empty space where a fridge could fit, but there was nothing there.

He stopped, electrified by a sudden thought. The clinic had been shut down before his mom came to town. Could the mayor have used the empty clinic to do his blood doping? Tor ducked into the room and stood, thinking. It made sense. The clinic had examining tables and a fridge to store the blood. This was the logical place for Mayor Malone to take blood from the snowboarding team. Then when his mom came to town, they realized they had to move. Mayor Malone had taken the entire refrigerator and hidden it in his office.

Tor imagined Brian Slader lying on the patient table in front of him. He imagined Mayor Malone leaning against the sink as he drained Brian's blood into a bag.

There really are vampires in the world, after all, Tor thought grimly.

Would there be evidence here? Fingerprints, blood, anything?

He quietly shut the door and started looking on the floor, on the patient table, and on the windowsill. He opened the doors over the sink and saw an array of bandages and swabs and tongue depressors. Each of the drawers opened to his touch but was empty or held nothing but more medical supplies. Tor took a pair of examining gloves from a drawer and, feeling kind of silly, put them on. He continued to the last drawer, which held nothing but dust, and then turned to the garbage can. He pulled it out to examine the contents just like he'd seen in television shows, and that was when he saw something underneath the cabinet, behind where the garbage can usually rested.

He squatted down and peered in. There was a piece of paper there, folded in half. It didn't look very large. He picked it up and opened it carefully.

It was a receipt, he saw with disappointment. Just a receipt for a purchase of a box of Safe-Paks, whatever they were, from some company back East somewhere. The logo of the company was a picture of something, and then Tor realized what it was: Safe-Paks were blood bags. He was holding a receipt for blood bags. His pulse started to pound.

Mayor Malone's fingerprints had to be on this

receipt. Tor knew that the lab people could get finger-prints off of anything—he'd seen a TV show once where they found fingerprints on someone's *eyeballs*.

Tor held his breath. He imagined how it had been tossed in the wastebasket and had slipped out, falling down behind. He knew the clinic didn't do blood dona-tions, at least not since his mom had come to town. Tor held the paper up to the light, trying to see the whorls of a fingerprint.

"What are you doing?"

Tor leaped to his feet. Mrs. Colm was in the doorway, her beady eyes looking from Tor to the paper in his hand. She'd never believe him—and if she touched the paper, he'd lose the fingerprints. He grabbed the end of the glove where he held the slip of paper, reversed it over the paper, and pulled it off his hand. The receipt was now safely inside the latex glove, with the fingerprints protected. Hopefully. He shoved it into his jacket pocket.

"Give me that," Mrs. Colm said, her voice angry and shaking at the same time. Tor looked wildly around the room. There was no way out. He didn't think. He launched himself at Mrs. Colm. She squawked and leaped backward as Tor pushed by her. She tried to grab onto him, to hold him. Her fingernails scrabbled on the smooth sleeve of his coat and then he tore free and he was running down the hallway toward the clinic door.

His mother was in the back with a patient, and he knew he wouldn't be able to find her before Mrs. Colm had the paper from him. He banged out the clinic doors, picked up his snowboard, and set off at a run toward the lodge and the chairlift. The receipt in its twist of glove felt like a burning coal against his chest.

Evidence, he thought, as he dodged his way through slow-moving people in the lodge and headed for the chairlift, his eyes searching the crowd for the familiar yellow-green of Raine's coat. Drake's dull brown colors were so neutral he'd never be able to find him. Raine would be the one to spot.

He found coats. They were blue. Jeff Malone and Max Nye stood holding their snowboards, chatting with a couple of cute girls. They weren't in the lift line, but were off to one side. Maybe Mrs. Colm had warned them, and they were waiting for him. Maybe they were just there to have fun. Either way, if they saw Tor, he'd be in for it.

Tor held his breath and joined the lift line, keeping his head turned away and using other riders to block him from the two older boys as he scrambled into his bindings. Drake and Raine had already taken the chairlift up. They must have, or he would have seen them by now.

Tor was almost at the front of the lift line when Jeff finally spotted him.

"Hey!" Jeff said, turning away from the girls and pointing at Tor. "Hey, waster! Hey! I wanna talk to you!"

Tor hopped up and let the chairlift scoop him up,

sighing as he was lifted into the air and away from Jeff and Max, who were now struggling to cut in line. A huge snowboarder with a black coat and a black helmet put a burly arm out and stopped them. As Tor was lifted up the mountain, he watched, grinning, as Jeff and Max had to take a place at the back of the line.

His friends weren't at the top of the lift, though. Tor stood with one foot out of his board, trying to decide what to do. Were they at the top of the second lift, at the terrain park? Where were they? His heart pounded and his mouth was dry. Skiers and snowboarders came off the chairlift like cakes off the end of an assembly line, some crashing and some gliding smoothly, and Tor knew it was only a matter of minutes before Jeff and Max were going to come off that line, too.

He made up his mind. He'd been down the upper slope once, and he hadn't been killed. Well, just barely not killed. He'd been working hard every day with Gloria, and if Drake and Raine were up at the top level at the terrain park, they'd let him follow them down the hill. He'd be with his friends, and if the worst happened, he'd pass the glove and the receipt to Drake and let Drake get it to Ms. Adams.

Tor skated over to the other lift line and got on the chair, panting. He was scared, that was the flat-out truth. He felt like he was going to throw up. He had the one piece of evidence that would clear his mom's name, and there was no way he was going to give it up even if he was afraid. He'd die before he'd hand it over like some tame little rabbit. Gloria had told him he had courage, he reminded himself as the lift line took him up to the top of the clouds. The silent woods of Raine's mountain stretched to his left. Time to show courage, if he had it.

He slid off the chairlift line and remained upright. He barely thought about it. He strapped in and rode over to the group at the terrain park. The board was such a part of him now he was only vaguely aware of what he was doing. Everyone at the terrain park was watching a kid dressed in screaming plaid make a leap and slide over some exposed railings. The rider scraped over the rail, hopped off the end, gave a whoop, and then fell in a spectacular flurry of snow and plaid. A single glove came off and spun circles in the sky before falling down and landing with a tiny puff of snow.

"Yard sale!" someone called out. The plaid rider got up, caked with snow, and laughed. He gave a bow and went sliding downhill to find his lost glove.

Raine wasn't there. Neither was Drake. Tor felt his stomach sink as he looked over the group again. And again. His friends weren't there. He fumbled his park map out of his jacket pocket and opened it with shaky fingers. He found the terrain park, the bowl they called Lucky Charms, and the two blocked avalanche chutes called the White Gates. The gate that he'd nearly gone into a few weeks ago was the Right Gate, which curved into Borsh Mountain land and began and ended in a crossed-poles symbol that meant danger—rocks, or something. The other gate was to the left of the terrain park. It was marked with the crossed poles as well. They looked like a crossbones symbol without the skull.

The terrain under the chairlift looked like it was okay. Tor thought he could make it down. He was a better snowboarder now, and he wasn't going to let Jeff and Max scare him. He could always try to follow their old trail and find the otters and their valley, if it came to that. He put the map back in his pocket, took a last look for Drake and Raine, and gave a hop so he could start gliding toward the enormous pylons that supported the chairlift.

The slope was still the same—like trying to snowboard off the side of a building. But his board seemed to grip better this time, and the slope didn't seem so terrible. He'd ridden through a pine forest, after all, he reminded himself, and the solution to any problem was to take it slowly and carefully.

He glided across the narrow slope and flipped the back end of his snowboard to come around and slide down around one of the big concrete pylons that supported the chairlift. Just as he came around the pylon, his board floating in the deep snow like a dream, he caught a glimpse of brilliant blue and clenched his jaw tight. Jeff. Max. No way he was going to panic now. He flipped again and headed back toward the trees, keeping his board cutting deep into the powdery snow. That was when Jeff Malone shot by him and smacked him hard in the back with an outstretched arm.

"Waster!" snarled Jeff, as Tor felt his board shoot across the slope, instantly going too fast to control. Jeff knew just what to do to make another snowboarder crash. He was going to give Tor another Snow Park Swirlie if he could, one that would probably put him in his mother's clinic with a broken leg or worse. But Tor knew about trees now. They were killers, all right, but he knew you could thread through them. He let his board go between the trees. He'd find a place to turn and then he could come out onto the slope and he'd be in control.

The trees were dense, but he avoided them the way Drake and Raine had showed him. Suddenly he thumped over plastic orange fencing buried in the deep snow and nearly lost his balance. Pinwheeling his arms, gasping, he abruptly shot out into an area completely free of trees.

Tor felt a burst of triumph as he turned downslope. He was suddenly in the clear and there were no trees. The snow was deep and fresh and there were no ski tracks or snowboard tracks at all. He should have realized this meant something. He didn't.

There was an open path in front of him and no Jeff and no Max—that was what mattered to Tor—and his snowboard floated across the unmarked snow like a dream.

He turned at the edge of the trees and continued down the slope, and that was when he heard the shouts of Jeff and Max. He could see their blue coats against the dark green of the pine trees. They were stopped at the edge of the open area and they were shouting and waving at him.

They don't sound angry, Tor thought distantly as he turned again in the deep narrow chute. The slope was so steep he was using everything he had to keep upright. Tor heard their shouts grow more frantic as he went downslope, and it was only at the last moment that he realized what they were shouting. They were shouting *stop*. They were shouting *please*. They were screaming *no*.

Tor was in one of the White Gates. He knew what the crossed poles on the map meant as he saw the cliff edge approaching. He threw his board into a heel-side position, but there was no stopping him. He flew out into space and had a final thought as he started to fall. He was kind of pleased about it.

No one else had done what he'd just done. He had just ridden the White Gate.

13 ☠ AVALANCHE CHUTE

THE FALL TOOK only seconds, but it seemed like a lot longer. Tor windmilled his arms, trying to keep upright. His heart climbed right up into his throat and stayed there, beating frantically, and he kept breathing in but couldn't seem to breathe out. The trees flashed by; first the tops, then the increasing width of the branches, then the trunks. He couldn't see anything beneath him, because he didn't look.

His board disappeared into snow and Tor followed. Then the snow gripped his body and he stopped with a jar that shook him from his head to his toes. Tor saw sparks and stars in front of his eyes and a darkness like curtains flapping in front of him.

He breathed out, and then breathed in again with a wheeze, and the stars and curtains started to fade. Tor panted and looked around, his board buried and his body upright. He was stuck like a toothpick into the snow all the way up to his armpits. Trees crowded close on each side, covered in white and showing only flashes of green needles and brown trunks. Tor looked over his head and saw a sheer cliff face above him that was so high he nearly started seeing stars again.

He'd stopped before he hit the rocks that were probably inches underneath his board. All the heavy snow that they'd had lately had piled up so deeply it made his landing a big soft pillow. Tor started working himself up out of the snow, hearing himself making a chuckling sound under his panting breath. He didn't like the sound; he sounded like a little kid getting ready to cry.

His snowboard came free and Tor laid back, arms spread-eagled like he was going to make a snow angel, feeling sweaty and hot. His heart still pounded hard but it was back down in his chest now, and his breathing was better. That odd noise he'd been making seemed to be done with for now, too.

Suddenly there was a piercing siren in the distance. Tor sat bolt upright. He'd never heard anything like it before. It was high and shrieking and said *Danger!* as clearly as someone screaming out loud. He looked wildly left and right, scooping some stray snow from the front of his goggles, but he didn't see anything.

Then he realized he was feeling something. The snow was trembling under his legs and backside. Earthquake! Tor gathered his legs close to himself, wondering what to do and where to go. The trembling increased, and Tor realized he was hearing a sound over the shrieking of the siren from the town. The sound was distant and rumbling, coming closer by the second, a sound like an ocean wave crashing toward shore.

This wasn't an earthquake. This was an avalanche. The siren was to warn the town that an avalanche was coming. And Tor realized with a sick feeling that he was sitting at the bottom of one of the avalanche chutes. The White Gates were avalanche chutes.

"Stop, stop, please!" Jeff and Max had yelled, their screams echoing off the snow-filled avalanche chute. Tor saw in his mind the echoing sound of their yells, bouncing off the walls of heavy snow that had been building for weeks. Their shouts had started the avalanche. The snow was coming right at him.

Tor started scooting backward toward the cliff face, his snowboard digging into the snow. Perhaps if he got right up at the edge of the cliff, the avalanche would fall over like a waterfall and he would be safe behind it. It wasn't much of a chance, but it was all he had. He'd seen avalanche footage on a snowboarding video that Drake had brought over to show him. Drake's dad and his cameraman had boarded safely away from an avalanche as the other camera had caught the gigantic cliff of snow breaking away and sliding downhill, gathering up pine trees like they were miniature toys and smashing down toward the valley floor below.

The rumbling was getting louder, and the shaking stronger. In just a few seconds a wave of snow was going to break over the cliff and bury everything underneath it in snow. Tor bumped up against the rocks at the cliff edge and felt a stinging as a sharp rock smashed into his back. He looked wildly around, trying to find a deeper spot where he could wedge himself, and saw an opening between two rocks. He shoved his way between the rocks and lifted his snowboard straight up and down so he could unclip the bindings and kick it away. If he got rid of his snowboard, he might be able to squeeze between the rocks and hide.

The entire world was shaking around him, worse than any earthquake he'd ever been in, worse than any earthquake on any movie he'd ever seen. His teeth were chattering and his fingers wouldn't take hold of the bindings, and he jammed his back harder against the cliff wall. Suddenly two enormous boulders of snow exploded over the cliff edge and came rocketing toward the earth below.

The earth behind him moved and Tor moved with it, shoving himself backward as though he was trying to dig into the cliff. Then, just as he realized what he was feeling wasn't rock but wood, the wood gave a cracking sound and fell away. Tor fell backward into blackness, his snowboard following him, and landed hard on his back inside an opening in the cliff.

Stars and sparks shot across his vision again and this

time he heaved for breath, without doing much good. The breath had been completely knocked out of him, and for a moment or two all he could do was try to get his lungs to work again. He was still trying to get some air when the rest of the avalanche came roaring over the cliff. Avalanche snow wasn't powdery and smooth. It was hard and full of trees and rocks. The remnant of a pine tree smashed down right in front of Tor. It was destroyed, split into shredded bark and broken branches. Abruptly it was swept away by more snow.

Tor scrambled backward, digging his board into the floor, as more and more snow shook the earth and thundered down, right where Tor had been standing before he fell. Another pine tree fell into the opening in front of him. Suddenly a massive downpour of snow crushed it. Tor could hear the cracking of the trunk and the splintering of the branches, as though the snow was eating the pine tree alive. It would have been him, if he'd still been standing against the cliff. A juicy smell burst from the tree as it gave up all its sap, and Tor threw his arms over his face as splinters shot into the cave entrance and pelted him. His helmeted head hit the floor with a smack and everything went away for a while.

A long time later Tor sat up. The tree was gone and there was nothing in the entrance but white that was rapidly turning to a dark gray. He felt a stinging on his forehead and reached up. A splinter was stuck straight into his head and Tor thought crazily for a second that he'd been impaled. The splinter fell out of his forehead as he touched it and he realized it had just scratched him. There was a sticky wetness on his face but there wasn't much of it. He gave a shaky laugh and then stopped, because he didn't like the sound.

His fingers finally stopped trembling, and he managed to unclip his snowboard. He stood up carefully and stepped toward the gray oval that was the cave entrance. He touched the snow with his gloved fingers. It felt as hard as iron. It was more ice than snow. Tor remembered the enormous pine tree that had been crushed into pine-tree jelly right in front of him, and felt a shiver that he stopped at once. If he was going to get out of here, he couldn't start panicking now.

He leaned his board against the cave wall and realized he was terribly thirsty. Scooping snow from his board, he held it in his mouth until it melted. There were granola bars in his pockets, he remembered.

And also Raine's flashlight. With a burst of relief he slapped his pockets and felt the reassuring roundness of her light. In a moment he had it out of his pocket and turned it on.

The darkness lit up around him, and Tor stood staring in wonder. He wasn't standing in a cave. He was standing in a tunnel, with sturdy timbers bracing the walls and a hard-packed floor underneath him.

"This is a mine," Tor said to himself, and heard his

voice echo behind him. He turned and looked down the tunnel. The light disappeared into inky blackness. This could only be one thing. This was the Borsh mine. Raine's great-great-great-grandfather's mine. Tor remembered how no one went on Borsh land, because there were too many dangerous mine shafts. Mr. Ewald had fallen into one, and a hiker had lost his life. The flashlight trembled in Tor's hands as he looked down the blackness of the mine tunnel.

He turned back to the oval entrance and wondered if anyone knew he was there. Had Jeff and Max told anyone? Would they call rescuers and try to dig him out? Or were they high-fiving each other right now, knowing their problem was solved?

Tor felt his jaw muscles clench. He touched his jacket and felt the outline of the blood bag receipt, safe in its latex glove. There was no way he was going to let them win. He picked up his snowboard and turned his flashlight so that it shone deeper into the tunnel. The floor looked level and clean, almost as though it had been swept, and the timbers that supported the walls seemed thick and well braced.

"Okay, Mr. Borsh, I'm counting on you," Tor said, and heard his voice go ahead of him into the darkness. He followed.

He found the first intersection a long time later. He had no idea how deep into Borsh Mountain he'd gone, or even if he was going straight into it. The air was as still as a held breath. He contemplated the inky blackness that waited in four directions. He sat down for a bit and ate a granola bar and scooped some more snow from his snowboard. He'd started forward again when he remembered that he had to mark his trail. He tore the empty granola bar wrapper in half and set it in the middle of the tunnel that led back. He found a small rock to hold it down. The tunnel was so clean and neat he had trouble finding even a small rock, and the thought of round Mr. Borsh sweeping his tunnel with a broom was so funny Tor laughed again. This laugh sounded stronger, more sure.

He decided to take the right turn, just because it sounded good. He walked down the tunnel and noticed his flashlight beam was getting a bit yellow. He tried to keep the panic down, but it nibbled at him like rats with sharp teeth. He could die in here, he knew that. There was no point in dwelling on it. After the third intersection of passageways, he started tearing his granola bar wrapper into small shreds so he'd have enough pieces of paper.

There was nothing in the mine but clean-swept floors, timbers, and dirt. Tor was running out of granola bar wrapper when he realized there was something ahead of him. The yellowing beam of the flashlight didn't quite reach whatever it was, and Tor stopped, uneasy. There was something on the floor of the mine ahead of him and it felt familiar. Strangely familiar.

He stepped closer, gripping his snowboard hard in one mitten and holding the flashlight hard in the other. The thing on the floor of the mine didn't move as he approached it.

Then he was in front of it, and his flashlight fell out of his suddenly boneless fingers and thumped dully on the thick softness of a woven blanket. Tor crouched down on one knee, and then he was sitting on the floor, his snowboard on his lap.

After a long time, he found his voice.

"Hello, Grandma," he whispered.

Leaping Water was perfectly preserved in the dry tunnel. She sat cross-legged, her beautiful deerskin dress faded to a vanilla yellow in the fading glow of the flashlight, her head bent down as though in thought. Tor couldn't see her face. Her white hair was braided the same way Raine liked to do, lying long and thick down her shoulders. She was seated on a soft woven blanket, and she had on deerskin moccasins that were covered with beads that glinted deep red, purple, and green in the glimmering light.

Tor didn't feel frightened at all. This was no corpse from a zombie movie. Leaping Water looked as peaceful and serene as though she'd just gone to sleep a little while ago. Next to her was a small scrap of paper that held within it the remains of what looked like bread and perhaps some kind of fruit. All that was left were dry withered twists. On the other side was a lantern.

Tor stared at this for several minutes before his brain figured out what he was looking at. He leaned forward. Could it still have fuel in it? After all these years?

"Grandma, can I use this?" he asked politely. She didn't object, so Tor reached forward and picked up the lantern. It sloshed, sounding full, and Tor sighed happily as he saw a package of matches tucked in the wire that held the lantern glass. He took it out and read out loud: "Borsh's General Store."

The matchbook held one match. Tor was careful with the lantern, taking the globe off and removing the small brass cap that covered the wick. The sharp smell of kerosene filled the tunnel. Tor struck the match and when the wick caught fire, he felt a burst of happiness. He sat back and turned off the flashlight and then adjusted the wick so the lantern gave off a steady light.

Then he took out a granola bar. It didn't seem odd to offer Grandma a bar, though she had no interest in it.

"We found the otters," Tor told her. He took a bite of his granola bar. "Your people. I'm so glad you didn't sell the land. That you kept it for the river people. We watched them. Did you know they like to play in the snow?"

Of course, Grandma replied in amusement. *I watched them for years.*

"Yeah, I know. I bet they're even better in the summertime, to watch I mean. I bet they play all day."

All day, Grandma said. *They love to play.*

"So I'm the doctor's son," Tor said finally, scooping a last bit of snow from his snowboard and putting it in his mouth. "I guess you knew that. Is that why I'm here?"

That is why you're here, Grandson, Grandma said. *Yes. That is why you're here.*

"Well, okay," Tor said. "What do you want me to do?"

But Grandma was silent on this. She looked down in her lap, as she had done for the past fifty years or so, and finally Tor realized she was trying to tell him something.

Her hands rested on something in her lap.

The something was an envelope, and Tor knew what it was.

"That's the deed, isn't it?" he asked.

Yes, it is, Grandma said. *You may take it.*

"Okay," Tor said. He felt nervous about touching Leaping Water, but only because he didn't want to disturb her. The envelope was thick and yellow, and as Tor pulled gently at the corner he touched her and she jingled musically. There were bells sewn into her hair braids and her deerskin dress.

"I bet you were great to know," Tor said. He tasted salt and realized his cheeks were wet. "Your great-granddaughter is terrific, too. Your whole family, actually."

You missed a few greats in there, I think, Grandma said. *But yes, I know.*

Tor looked inside the envelope and saw the thick parchment. *Mining Deed of Trust,* he read, and felt a light bloom inside him that was stronger than the kerosene lamp.

"Thanks," he said. There didn't seem to be anything else to say.

The envelope went into his jacket pocket, where it rested next to the blood bag receipt. Tor remembered a high-wire act he'd once seen, where the artist carried a long pole. On one side was a tea tray complete with a steaming teapot and on the other was a small poodle dog dressed like a clown. The burden was just too ridiculous to be believed. Tor touched his jacket and remembered how the artist crossed the wire with small, careful steps.

"One step at a time," Tor muttered to himself, and he set off down the passageway in the direction he'd been going when he'd met Grandma. This had to be the way out. The envelope crackled in his pocket, and the lantern was warm and lit up the whole passageway.

But the tunnel ended in a blank wall.

Tor stood for a long time, wondering what was going on. He had the deed, Grandma Leaping Water had shown him where to go—where was the door?

He put down his snowboard and pushed and prodded at the wall. Maybe there was a secret door there? A secret exit? The wall was rough and seemed to be made up of hardened dirt, not stone. Tor pushed harder at the dirt, but it acted just like dirt and nothing happened.

Tor finally turned around and sat down, thumping

his back against the wall. He'd been so sure! Exhaustion suddenly rose up in him. His eyes were sore, his head hurt, his throat was raw, and he was thirsty again. He'd ridden the White Gates, he'd fallen off a cliff, he'd escaped an avalanche and found Leaping Water and her deed, and after all of that he was going to die here. For nothing. He put his head down on his knees and clutched his helmeted head with both hands, and he put every ounce of will into not crying.

Eventually Tor got up and walked back down the passageway. There didn't seem to be anything else to do. After a few minutes Grandma appeared in the lantern light, waiting, eternally serene. Tor sat down next to her and leaned against the wall. He set his board down and turned his head to look at her.

"Well, unless you have any other ideas," he said, "I'm fresh out."

Grandma remained silent.

Tor let his head rest against the wall. It was cold in there, but not freezing. His snowboarding gear kept him comfortable. He let his eyes close, just for a moment, to try to collect his thoughts.

When he opened them, he couldn't figure out where he was. His head ached, his body hurt everywhere, and his mouth was dry and sticky. Everything was blurry. He moved, groaned, and finally sat up.

He'd been resting on the edge of Grandma Leaping Water's blanket. For a moment Tor remembered with perfect clarity that he'd been dreaming of the otters. Grandma had been an otter, so full of life and fun that she splashed like liquid sunlight as she romped in and out of the river, and he'd been running after her on his four clever feet, his tail bumping and his whiskers twitching, making a yipping sound of happiness before he plunged into the cool stream water. . . .

Then the dream was gone like smoke because the lantern was guttering. He'd been asleep and he'd *left the lantern on.* He had no more matches and the flashlight was just about dead. The lantern, his only light, was about to go out and leave him forever in the dark.

14 ☠ STAIRWAY

TOR LEAPED TO his feet, his heart kicking in his chest like an animal trying to tear its way out of a cage. He snatched up the lamp and it was so hot he nearly lost his grip and dropped it. He clutched the handle in his hands and bit back a whimper. How long had he been asleep?

Grandma Leaping Water still sat, as she always would, peaceful and quiet in her nest of blankets. Just looking at her steadied Tor. There had to be more than one entrance and exit to the mine tunnels. He'd just have to find another way.

The flame guttered in the lamp as if it was mocking him, and he willed it to keep burning. It guttered again, the flame almost torn from the wick in the breeze coming down the passageway.

Tor blinked, and realized what he was seeing. The wick was streaming back because there was a *breeze*.

Somewhere there was fresh air blowing into the mine. He turned without taking his eyes from the wick and tried to see where the breeze was coming from.

It was coming down the same tunnel he'd gone down hours before, the one that ended in a blank wall. He must have missed something, some side tunnel perhaps. He set the lamp down and picked up his snowboard, and then he turned to Leaping Water.

"Is this the right way?"

The amused, young-sounding voice that he'd heard in his head hours ago didn't come back. Maybe he'd imagined the whole conversation. Tor tapped his finger at his chest and felt the crackle of parchment. He hadn't imagined the envelope. He picked up the lantern by the wire handle and walked down the tunnel, lamp held high, snowboard gripped in his other hand.

There were no side tunnels. The lamp took him to the same dirt wall. The lamplight glowed across it and showed Tor nothing but brown stuff that smelled bitter and dank. He stared at the lamp, willing it to show him where the breeze was coming from, but it guttered a final time, the flame was torn from the wick, and the light was drowned by darkness.

Tor stood for what seemed like a long time, stupidly willing the lamp to relight, but it hung from his hand silently. It was now nothing but a cooling lump of metal. He shook it and heard no sloshing sound. He set the lamp carefully on the ground. He put down his snowboard, resting it against one wall, and it was only then as he made sure it wasn't going to fall over that he realized that he could see his snowboard. And he had seen the lamp when he put it down.

Tor looked around wildly. There was light coming from somewhere. It was coming from the dirt wall in front of him. There was a crack, thin as a silver wire. Tor got to his hands and knees, and a cold breeze blew on his face as he tried to see what was beyond the crack. He couldn't see anything, but he could tell the crack led to something and there was light in there. It had to be a way out.

He sat down on the tunnel floor and kicked at the crack with all his might. The impact jarred him to the top of his aching head and he groaned. He kicked again, this time lying on his back and scooting close to the wall so he could kick with all his strength. After the third kick, when he knew he couldn't do it anymore, he felt something give way.

There was a sound like a branch snapping, and his boot was suddenly calf-deep in the wall. Tor pulled his foot away carefully and got up to look through the hole he'd made. There was nothing but dazzling whiteness. Tor couldn't see trees or snow, and somehow it didn't look like open air. Whatever it was, there was light in there. He sat down again and kicked at the edge of the hole. This time an entire section broke free and Tor scrambled backward as dirt and white rock came thudding down. Choking gray dust filled the air, and Tor coughed and moved backward down the tunnel, waiting for the air to clear.

When it did, Tor nearly whooped out loud with joy. There was a boy-sized opening in the wall. Light and fresh cold air poured through the hole. Tor carefully scrambled through and pulled his snowboard after him. He stood up and looked around. He had no idea where he was.

He was standing in a small room. There was a wall in front of him, a wall that looked like it was made of grayish-white clouds. There was a silver ladder bolted to the wall.

Tor contemplated this for a while. Finally he stepped forward carefully and looked to make sure the ladder didn't lead downward, too. Then he looked up. He didn't know what he was going to see, and he was more than a little afraid.

Far above him there was a square hatch. Pure light outlined the hatch and flooded down into the room where he stood. Tor put a hand out and touched the gray wall. It felt like concrete, cold and smooth, and it curved slightly as though he was standing in front of some huge column buried in the earth. The other walls in this strange room were also painted gray. Tor looked back at the hole he'd crawled through and saw chunks of plaster on the ground. His breath smoked in the cold air and drifted upward toward the hatch.

The ladder was solid and just as real as the walls. Finally he tucked his snowboard under his arm and put his hands on the ladder. The hatch had to be the way out.

He started to climb. Halfway up, the ladder began to thrum like a plucked guitar string. Tor almost lost his grip. He clung to the ladder, panting, the thrumming sound making his very bones vibrate. He forced himself to keep going, though he was shaking. He shoved away the tiny, miserable thought that he'd had enough already, that somebody should help him, that he was only a kid and he'd gone through too much to go on. Thinking like that was halfway to giving up, and Torin Sinclair didn't give up.

"Torin Sinclair always gets back up," Tor muttered to himself, and he reached the hatch at last.

The hatch looked very ordinary. It was made of a shiny metal, and there was a latch and a handle so a person underneath could lift it. Tor rested his snowboard on his knees, took a deep breath, and tried to open it. It resisted, and he braced himself and shoved, hard. The hatch opened.

He climbed out into blazing sunshine and deep white snow. Tor sat on the edge of the hatch, his eyes smarting in the light, and realized he had been climbing a ladder on the side of a huge gray tower, a column of concrete. He followed the tower up to the sky and saw cables, and then he saw the chairlifts go sailing smoothly by and the tower thrummed as the chairs thumped over its support bars.

He'd found his way to a chairlift pylon. He'd been at the bottom of the pylon, buried deep in the earth, and he'd climbed up the mechanic's access ladder. The hatch was sheltered by an overhang and surrounded by padding, but some snow still blew in and that was what he'd had to move when he'd opened the hatch.

He was back on Snow Mountain. Tor felt something inside him come bubbling out. It was laughter, and he let it go free. He laughed and laughed, holding his snowboard in his hands, his feet still dangling in the hatch, and the blue sky overhead was the most beautiful sight he'd ever seen. He was alive. And he was sitting right next to a chairlift pylon on the groomed slope of the Snow Park resort.

Tor put his goggles on. He closed the hatch and climbed the protective orange padding that surrounded the pylon. He'd never looked closely at a pylon before. He'd always just avoided them like everyone else did. Now Tor could see that the padding surrounded the pylon and the access hatch. Once he was up and over the padding, Tor could see the slope and the town below. He sat in the snow for a moment and just looked at it.

Snow Park had never looked so pretty. The roofs were covered in snow and the streets sparkled in the sun. Cars drove down Main Street, heading toward the resort parking lot. The resort must have just opened, because only a few coats were milling down by the chairlift and the parking lots were just starting to fill up. The lodge looked busy, with lots of people wearing red Ski Patrol jackets standing outside.

To his left and just downslope was a small warming hut and snack bar. Tor had never been in there. It was used mostly by small kids and their parents, who needed to warm up and let the little kids take breaks.

They serve hot chocolate, Tor thought, and his stomach growled savagely at him. A single hot chocolate, he thought, and then he remembered what he carried.

If he was caught before he found his mom, or Drake and Raine, he'd lose the evidence he'd nearly died to save. No matter how cold and hungry he was, his job wasn't done.

Tor sat and worked his boots into his snowboard bindings, clipped in, and hopped to his feet. He glided downslope. The cold air bit at his exposed nose and cheeks but it felt great.

He had to keep that paper safe and get it into safe hands. Tor stopped to settle his goggles around his eyes. He looked up at the chairlift, wishing with all his heart that he would see Drake and Raine up there.

And there they were. Tor nearly fell down. Raine was on the chairlift, wearing her yellow-green coat. Drake was right next to her, his mittens clutching the lift bar and his head thrust forward from his shoulders like he was trying to get the chairlift to hurry up. Tor filled his eyes with the sight of them, his friends. They were coming to look for him.

"Hey!" he shouted. "Raine! Drake! Hey!"

They turned their heads toward him slowly, as though they were wondering if they were dreaming. Tor shouted again and waved both arms, laughing.

"It's me! It's Tor!" he shouted. "I've got the proof! I'm alive and I've *got the proof*!"

Three chairs ahead of Drake and Raine, someone turned abruptly and looked at Tor. There was Deputy Rollins, now dressed as Coach Rollins in snowboarding pants and an electric blue jacket. He stared at Tor, his face white and grim, and the look on Rollins's face told him everything he needed to know. Tor had been wrong the whole time. The vampire wasn't Mayor Malone, after all. The vampire was Rollins.

Tor looked back at Drake and Raine, and they were looking at Rollins, too. It was so obvious now. Rollins had been the one who was blood doping the team. He had everything to lose if his secret was found out. He'd lose his coaching position, his job, and his reputation. He was Coach Rollins of the Snow Park snowboarding team, the team that won championships, and Tor knew his secret. Tor knew that Rollins had taken too much blood from Brian Slader and had killed him. If Rollins caught Tor, he would never make it off the mountain alive. And Rollins was about to get off the chairlift.

"Tor, go, go!" Raine screamed from the chairlift.

Drake was already pulling his goggles down, and both of them were shoving their free feet into their snowboards, getting ready to exit the chairlift with both feet strapped in, a move that Gloria told Tor she'd rip his head off like a daisy if he ever tried.

Tor didn't wait to see if they made it off the lift. He turned and pointed his board straight downhill and rode for his life.

15 ☠ THE RACE

TOR HEARD MUSIC. He was making it. His snowboard cut through fresh powder with a sound like tearing paper, and as he switched back and forth to keep control, he heard the music of his board and he heard the music in his head. He knew he couldn't outrace Coach Rollins. He was just a kid and he hadn't been snowboarding very long.

But there was music in the way his board cut through the snow. There was music in the clear blue day and the sunlight. Tor felt no fear at all. Instead, he felt a goofy kind of happiness filling him. The sun was shining and the powder was perfect, his friends were coming, and his snowboard was singing the "Gloria" in Ms. Adams's song. The baritone was an easy part. Just a bunch of O's, like a snowboard gliding down a hill.

He would be at the bottom in a few minutes and he

shouldn't have wished it, but he found himself wishing the run were going to take longer.

Then Tor heard a panting like a wolf and the tearing-paper sound of a snowboarder coming fast. Rollins had caught up to him. Tor crouched down, trying to get more speed. His heart tried to climb up into his throat. His board was singing and he knew he was going to win. He had no idea how, but he knew he was going to win this race.

"Tor, go left!" Raine shouted from behind him, and without hesitation Tor threw his board to the left, toe-side into the mountain. He watched as the snow slid past his nose, and when he reached out a glove to steady himself, an arc of snow sprang up in a head-high spray. Rollins was a blue blur, coming fast. Tor crouched and headed straight for the trees. There was another path on the other side of the trees, a narrow glade called Moose Hollow, and he knew Rollins was forcing him in there because no one could see them from the resort. They'd be hidden until the bottom of the run, which emptied out directly in front of the lodge.

But Tor knew he had no choice. If he stopped now, Rollins would catch him and take his papers, his proof, and then no one would ever believe him. He had to beat Rollins to the lodge.

He rocketed between the trees and burst into the Hollow. Trees dotted the slope and powder sparkled on every branch. There were no tracks in the fresh snow, and it glittered at Tor like a million diamonds. He had to grin as his board floated into the powder and he curved around the first pine tree. The snow was *awesome*!

"Tor, right!" Raine screamed from somewhere behind him, and Tor instantly threw his board to the right, missing a tree by a millimeter. A cascade of snow fell from the tree, as though he'd startled it.

Then he saw Drake. Tor had never watched Drake ride. He'd never seen anyone ride like that before. Drake cut in front of Rollins, who threw his board into a turn that sent him toward the trees. Drake cut in front of him again, his board sending up a curve of snow like a surfer's wave. Rollins dodged again and Drake moved even before the bigger man had finished his turn, blocking him again. Tor saw Drake's teeth show in a grin that looked as sunny and innocent as a little kid's, and then Drake threw his board into the air right at Rollins, and Rollins turned desperately to avoid the impact.

Rollins went into the trees and Drake hit the branches of a pine tree. White snow cascaded down as Drake twisted in midair, flipped over, and came down on the slope. He was perfectly in control.

Tor had never seen anything so incredible. He knew he was grinning and laughing at the same time because his teeth were freezing. He turned his board downslope and kept going.

Raine was on the other side now, and the three of them raced together down the mountain. Tor heard the song inside his head, singing about mountains echoing in reply. He didn't realize he was singing out loud until Raine joined in.

"*Angels we have,*" she sang, and turned on her board as Tor and Drake turned, too, the three of them together.

"*Heard on high,*" she continued in her soprano voice. She was short of breath and panting, but she sounded beautiful.

"*Sweetly singing,*" Tor and Drake sang together, as they turned again on the slope.

"*O'er the plains,*" they sang together, and it wasn't nearly as good as everyone sounded in Ms. Adams's class, but Tor didn't care. It sounded great to him.

"*And the mountains in reply.*" They turned again, throwing sprays of white powder into the air in three perfect arcs.

"*Echoing their joyous strain.*" Tor couldn't help laughing as he heard their voices bounce off the slopes of the valley and, indeed, echo in reply. They all took a deep breath and came down the final slope, bursting out of the trees and racing toward a waiting crowd, and they were singing.

"*Glo-o-o.*" Tor lost the last section of O's because he started laughing again.

"*Ria. In excelsis deo.*" Tor picked up the last section with Drake and Raine and they came to a stop, spraying snow into the air from the edges of their snowboards.

Tor thought that definitely showed some attitude. He felt just fine about it.

Tor saw his mother, and there was Ms. Adams at the very front of the crowd. She stood with hands clasped and her mouth trembling, and she was crying but suddenly she was clapping her mittened hands together, banging them against each other. She was applauding.

Tor reached down to unclip his board. There were more people coming toward them, running, and some were running the other direction and shouting the news to people in the lodge. Tor was still unclipping when he sensed more than heard the sound behind him.

Drake and Raine, who'd unclipped faster than he had, were ready. They turned and held their snowboards like weapons, facing back upslope. Tor stepped out of his board and turned around to see Rollins coming downslope fast, his nose and chin covered with blood and his eyes blazing out of a furious white face.

"You stop!" Raine screamed, and jabbed her board toward Rollins. "You stop right now!"

"What's going on here?" someone asked behind Tor, and he turned around to see Mayor Malone standing next to his mother and Ms. Adams. The mayor was dressed in an enormous brown parka. His face was flushed pink with the cold and his mustache was frosted with ice.

"Left, Tor," Drake said casually, and Tor jumped to

his left. A split second later, Rollins came through the space where Tor had just been. Tor stood next to Drake and watched as Rollins tried to stop, overcorrected, and smashed to the ground at the feet of Mayor Malone. The mayor was spattered with snow. It was all very satisfying.

"If he's armed, we're toast," Drake said.

"You think he's that crazy?" Tor asked.

"Yeah, he's that crazy," Raine said in a perfectly conversational tone of voice. She moved to Tor's other shoulder and the three of them stood together. They waited, still panting, their snowboards upright and held at their sides.

"What's going on here?" Mayor Malone asked again, staring angrily down at Rollins. Rollins rolled over and groaned, then fumbled at the straps of his board.

"I have proof he was blood doping the snowboarding team," Tor said quickly, before the deputy could unstrap and get up. "That's why he's trying to hurt me. I've got the proof right here."

Tor patted his chest, and looked at Drake and then Raine and saw their stunned faces. They didn't know, he realized. They didn't know about the blood bag receipt, or Leaping Water in the mine, or any of it. They were protecting him and they didn't even know why. He felt a hitch in his stomach. Tor turned back to his mother, who looked shocked, then, with dawning comprehension, very angry.

"What are you talking about?" said Mayor Malone.

"Blood doping?" Dr. Sinclair said, shoving her way ahead of Mayor Malone. "Did you say blood doping?"

"Yes," Tor said. "I found a blood bag receipt and it has Deputy Rollins's fingerprints on it."

Tor suddenly became aware of a strange humming noise. It was the chairlift, rolling empty chairs up the mountain and circling them back down. There wasn't another sound. The crowd that surrounded them had gone absolutely silent. Plumes of white breath rose in the air from a hundred mouths, but no one said a word.

"That's why Brian Slader died," Tor said loudly, and his voice, maddeningly, trembled. He forced it lower so it wouldn't shake. "Deputy Rollins took too much of Brian's blood. We found blood bags. Blood bags with the snowboarding team's names on them. He takes blood from them and puts it back in before competitions so they can win. But he took too much blood from Brian."

"This story is crazy," Rollins said. He was on his feet and he had wiped the blood off his chin. He looked calm and grown-up, and Tor suddenly felt very small and very young. "This boy ran away from home. He caused the whole town to search for him for nothing, and now he shows up with some wild story."

"I didn't run away," Tor said. "I got chased into one of the White Gates. I went off the cliff. I was in the avalanche."

"No one could survive in the White Gates," sneered Deputy Rollins. "No one could survive an avalanche in the Gates. You're lying. You're a liar!"

"I found a mine shaft," Tor said. He glanced at Drake and Raine again and started grinning. He couldn't help it. That goofy happiness was filling him again. "I found one of the Borsh tunnels and I hid in that. It took me all night to find my way out. That's the truth."

There was a shifting murmur in the crowd, which seemed to be swelling by the second. Tor caught a glimpse of Gloria and she was smiling at him but her eyes were bloodshot and red. Could she have been searching for him, too? He knew that she had, as sure as the sky was blue. She'd been searching all night for him, while he was lost in the dark. She hadn't given up, and neither had Drake, or Raine, or his mother. They'd been looking for him. The whole town had been looking for him.

"That's a damned lie," Rollins said. "He comes to this town, his mother comes to this town, and people die. That's the truth. He sets off an avalanche that nearly kills two town kids—"

"They set it off!" shouted Tor.

"And now he claims he found the Borsh mine. You believe this? Anyone believe this pile of lies?"

"I have proof," Tor said, and the words silenced the swelling murmurs of the crowd of townspeople.

"Proof?" sneered Rollins. "What—" But he stopped, because Tor had drawn something from his pocket.

"These are matches from Borsh's General Store," he said. The hidden envelope stayed in his jacket, a warm secret like a heated coal. He held the box up in the air. "I found them in the mine."

It was as good as a magic trick, that tiny box. Tor could see the stunned expression on Rollins's face.

"My son is no liar," Dr. Sinclair shouted over the excited chatter that burst out. "I don't need to see proof to know that. And I'm a doctor. Brian Slader died from blood loss, not pulmonary edema. He died because he didn't have enough blood in his system. Rollins, have you been taking blood from your snowboarding team? Have you been *blood doping*?"

"I certainly have not!" Rollins shouted, and Tor heard the panicked lie in his voice as clearly as the ringing of a bell. The crowd murmured and shifted again and then fell silent. Tor saw people turning to look at a group wearing blue jackets. The snowboarding team stood, looking at the ground, saying nothing.

Tor looked at his friends. Drake was still holding his snowboard at the ready, shoulder to shoulder with Tor. Raine was at his other shoulder, her eyes glittering like black oil in the sunlight.

"We found a refrigerator from the clinic," Tor continued. "It was full of blood bags marked with team names. Then I found this." He reached into his jacket pocket and pulled out the receipt. It was wrapped in the glove. The glove looked small and pitiful and flabby in the clear morning air.

There was an uncomfortable silence. Tor swallowed hard.

"I'll take that," someone said, and Tor saw a man step out from behind Ms. Adams. He was wearing a heavy navy blue parka with a furry hood, and as he pulled the hood back Tor saw a tight-fitting blue cap on the man's head. The cap held a patch that shone with gold. It was a badge.

"It's about time," Drake murmured, and blew out a breath that sent a cloud of white vapor into the sky.

"Who are you?" Tor said, although his heart was already beating with hope.

"Ford Graham, Colorado Bureau of Investigation," the man said, and the words were the Excalibur sword that Tor wished he could have pulled from his jacket instead of the flabby little glove. Behind the CBI agent was Ms. Adams, who was nodding at Tor with a smile that made her look like a very satisfied little wood elf.

"I can take you to the blood, too," Tor said. "If they haven't moved it."

"We'll take a look," the man said. "I'm glad to see you're okay, son. We were worried about you. Can I have that evidence, please?"

Tor handed it over, and as he did he saw Rollins and

the expression on the deputy's face wasn't fearful at all. Tor felt his heart sink like a stone.

"You aren't getting anything off that paper!" Rollins hissed, in a voice so full of hatred that Tor felt Raine quiver next to him. "I wore gloves! You're not getting anything off that paper!"

Tor felt like he'd been punched in the stomach. All the work he'd done! The risk he'd taken to keep the receipt safe, all that he'd been through. He'd snowboarded off a cliff, he'd nearly died, and the paper had turned out to be worthless. There would be no fingerprints, no evidence for the jury, and no arrest. He'd failed.

Then he saw Deputy Rollins's expression. His face was shocked and he was no longer looking triumphant. He was instead looking at the CBI officer, who was staring back at him with an expression of profound satisfaction.

"Well, that was a stupid thing to say," Graham said, smiling. "And in front of witnesses, too. Sir, it doesn't matter if this receipt has fingerprints on it or not. With this, I can find out who *paid* for those blood bags. Care to let me know whose name I'm going to find at the end of that trail?"

Rollins looked down and wiped at his bleeding nose. He said nothing.

Mayor Malone stepped forward. Tor watched him. He'd thought the mayor was the killer the whole time, and he'd been wrong. The mayor was a creep, but he wasn't a murderer, and the look on the mayor's face said it all. His face was dead white. He looked sickened, as though he was about to throw up.

"You took blood from *my* son?" he said, his voice cracking. "You took my Jeff's *blood*?"

The mayor lunged toward Rollins but someone abruptly blocked his way. Sheriff Hartman had on a big hat and a dark brown parka with a shield pinned to the front, and his face looked more than ever like a mournful basset hound's.

"Move back, now, move back, Stanford," Sheriff Hartman said. His voice was as deep and sad as his face.

"Some detectives we turned out to be," Drake murmured to Tor, and he had to pretend to cough in order to keep from laughing out loud as the sheriff tried to keep the mayor from Deputy Rollins.

"Hold him," the CBI agent said to the sheriff. Then he took silver handcuffs from his pocket and said the magical words to Deputy Rollins that made Drake and Raine and Tor smile like they'd each gotten a brand-new snowboard on Christmas morning.

"You have the right to remain silent. . . ."

16 ☠ THE ENVELOPE

TOR'S MOM DIDN'T make a fuss over him, which was a relief. She stepped forward while Deputy Rollins was still being handcuffed and she took Tor by the arm.

"Let's go, Tor," she said in a low voice. "You too, kids."

Drake and Raine nodded and they followed her. A German shepherd dog lunged forward and sniffed Tor so enthusiastically he stumbled backward. The handler was smiling, and she reached down to pet the dog as it sniffed at Tor's legs.

"Give her just a second," the handler said. She was a weathered woman with deep wrinkles around her bloodshot eyes. Tor realized she'd been up all night searching for him, too. "We hardly ever find them alive, and avalanche dogs get awfully depressed. Saber here needs to know she's found her boy. Yes, you found him, good girl, good girl!"

The dog wagged her brushy tail back and forth joyfully as Tor reached down to let her sniff his hand, remembering what the pine tree had looked like as the falling avalanche crushed it. No, he didn't suppose that Saber often found avalanche victims alive.

"I'm getting him out of here," Dr. Sinclair said to Sheriff Hartman, who was trying to lean past her and catch Tor by the arm. The CBI agent, Mr. Graham, was busy with the deputy and the crowd was closing in: Gloria and her Ski Patrol friends, dressed in red and looking both exhausted and happy; Ms. Adams; Mr. Ewald, the math teacher.

Tor felt Drake and Raine behind him, pushing him toward Dr. Sinclair, and then they were walking through the lodge. Someone tried to take his snowboard from his arm and he jerked back fiercely, protectively. Then he realized it was Mr. Douglas, Raine's dad, who made a soothing gesture with his hands. Tor let the snowboard go. The street was too bright outside the lodge, and there were too many people crowding around. Mr. Douglas shoved ahead of them and opened a door, and Tor found himself walking up a flight of stairs, half-carried by strong arms. Things seemed too light and then too dark, but it didn't seem important to ask any more questions.

Someone pushed a hot drink into his hands.

"Drink it," his mother said gently, and Tor sipped at

it. It tasted strongly of honey but underneath was some kind of bitterness that didn't taste good at all.

"That's awful," he said, but Dr. Sinclair pushed it back into his hands.

"Drink some more, Tor," she commanded gently, and he gulped it grudgingly down. There were hands all over him, it seemed—pulling off his boots, taking off his helmet, tugging at his snowboarding jacket and pants.

"No signs of frostbite," he heard someone say, and realized it was Mr. Douglas. Something in the tea was bringing everything back into focus again. Tor was sitting on the couch in the Douglases' apartment, and his mother had him undressed to his thermal underwear.

"Hey!" he said, as he realized Grandma Douglas was watching him. She was sitting in a chair that Raine usually curled up in, looking no bigger than her granddaughter. Her black eyes crinkled as she smiled at him.

"He's not hurt a bit," she said to Dr. Sinclair.

"I think you're right," Dr. Sinclair said. She was feeling Tor's bare toes, examining them one by one with gentle hands. Mr. Douglas was also in the room, Tor saw. There was no one else there.

"Where's—" he began.

"In the kitchen, getting some food," Mr. Douglas said. He was looking at Tor's fingers with the same intensity Dr. Sinclair showed, examining each finger as though he was looking for something. "They're exhausted. They've been up all night waiting for word about you. We wouldn't let them on the mountain until this morning, which didn't sit well with either one of them."

"We practically had to sit on them to keep them from going up with the search party," Dr. Sinclair said. "It was a long night for us down here, Tor."

"I'm sorry," he said.

"Oh, don't say that," Dr. Sinclair said, and touched his toes very gently with her warm, strong hands. "No sorrys, no tears, not on this day. No frostbite here, not a sign. I'll keep an eye on your feet and hands for a few days to be sure, but there's no white or green patches, and you don't seem to be in any pain."

"The mine wasn't that cold, and I had my gear on," Tor explained as his mother took his head in her hands and started feeling through his hair.

"How did you get cut?" Dr. Sinclair asked, looking at Tor's forehead. He couldn't remember for a moment, then he did.

"The tree," he said. "When the avalanche crushed it, it shot splinters into the tunnel entrance. I fell back and hit my head—with my helmet on, Mom!" he said, annoyed, as Dr. Sinclair felt his head again.

"I'll get some fresh clothes for you, Tor," Mr. Douglas said. "Dr. Sinclair, the sheriff is going to want to take a statement from Tor."

"The CBI man will, too," Dr. Sinclair said, her lips

thinned. "He can just take Tor's statement right here. I won't let him take a sick boy to the police station."

"I'm not sick!" Tor protested.

"I think that's quite clear." Mr. Douglas grinned and left the room.

Dr. Sinclair pressed an icy stethoscope to Tor's chest. He gasped and then resigned himself as she listened to his lungs, felt his belly, and looked in his ears.

"Mom," he said finally.

She sat back on her knees and looked up at him. She was smiling. "I know, overkill. I just have to know you're okay. I thought you were dead, Tor. All night."

"I'm sorry," he said again, and his voice thickened so he cleared his throat.

"Don't be. It wasn't your fault," Dr. Sinclair said. "And I'm not going to wrap you up like a baby and keep you from that mountain and from your snowboard. I would never do that."

"I know," Tor said. He had never thought she would.

"I just would— I would have missed you, that's all," Dr. Sinclair said, and she sat down on the couch next to him and held him, hard, and she did cry a little, after all.

Mr. Douglas came into the room with an old pair of sweatpants and a soft jersey for Tor, and a box of tissues for Dr. Sinclair. He smiled and winked at her when he handed her the box. Tor pulled on the sweatpants and sat back down. Dr. Sinclair was blowing her nose when Drake and Raine pushed into the room, followed by

Mrs. Douglas and her young son. Behind them came the round form of Sheriff Hartman.

Tor was pulling on his jersey and froze, seeing the sheriff.

"Son, I need to take a statement," the sheriff said. He raised his hands in a peace gesture toward Tor, who sat back down on the couch. His sad hound eyes looked tired. Drake and Raine sat down firmly on either side of Tor. Dr. Sinclair stood up.

"You're not moving him," she told the sheriff. He sighed and looked around the room.

"The CBI agent is going to be here any minute. Let me know what happened so I know what's been going on with my deputy. Can you tell me that?"

"I . . . okay," Tor said.

"Start at the beginning," Sheriff Hartman said.

Tor started with the fridge full of blood. He had come up with a story already—he was looking for his mom, who wasn't at the office, and he knew that she and Mayor Malone had agreed to go out for coffee, so he went to the mayor's office looking for them.

"I was just wandering around looking for them," he said, as innocently as he could manage, "and I saw the fridge from the clinic in the back room. I knew it belonged in the clinic so I looked in it. I saw there were blood bags in there, so I left and talked to Drake and Raine about it."

He looked at Drake, then at Raine. They nodded, as

though they'd rehearsed the whole story and there was no nighttime break-in of the mayor's office.

"We spoke to Ms. Adams at the school," Tor said.

"Why Ms. Adams?" the sheriff asked. He had taken a seat and was writing in his notebook.

"Because she was friendly to me," Tor said. "Everyone else treated me like an outsider. Like I was cursed or something." He looked innocently at the sheriff and was pleased to see the big man shift his feet and look faintly ashamed.

"We couldn't trust the mayor because we—I—found the fridge in his office. And I was afraid to go to you."

"Deputy Rollins *was* my deputy," the sheriff said. "Notice the past tense. There's nothing worse, in my opinion, than a lawmaker who won't uphold the law. Where are you going to turn if the lawman is bad? You young folks decided you couldn't turn to me, so you talked to the choir teacher at the school. For heaven's sake, the *choir teacher.*"

"Yes, sir," Tor said slowly. If he'd gone to the sheriff, he'd never have found Leaping Water, either, or the—

"My jacket!"

"Right here, Tor," Raine said, picking it up from beside the couch. "What is it?"

"Later," Tor said, taking it in his hands and feeling the slight crackle of paper. "Later."

"Where did you go after Ms. Adams promised to bring in the CBI?"

"And here he is now," Mrs. Douglas said as the doorbell rang. "We're getting quite a crowd here. Hold on a moment."

Mrs. Douglas brought back the CBI agent, Ms. Adams, and Mayor Malone. In the meantime Raine pushed a turkey sandwich into Tor's hands, and he wolfed two enormous bites. He lifted the sandwich toward Ms. Adams in greeting as she entered and she smiled back at him. He didn't smile at Mayor Malone.

"Here's the choir teacher," Sheriff Hartman said, standing up and hitching at his heavy belt. He reached forward to shake hands with the mayor, the CBI agent, and finally Ms. Adams. "The most trusted woman in town, I hear."

Ms. Adams lifted her chin until she looked as regal as a tiny queen.

"That's what I hear, too," she said. "I trust you'll forgive me for not coming to you?"

"Having the CBI called in over my head isn't my favorite moment as a lawman, frankly," said the sheriff. He nodded coolly at the CBI agent.

"I had three young people put their trust in me," Ms. Adams said, a red blush climbing her neck, her chin held even higher. "Their lives were at risk. I did what I felt I had to do."

"There's no blame attached to this," the CBI agent said, his face as calm and still as a carved block of granite. "Ms. Adams did the right thing, and so have you, sir. We have Rollins in custody and the evidence safely in hand, and no one's been hurt. You're not hurt, are you, son?"

"Nope," Tor said.

"I'm Mr. Graham, Tor. I'm very glad to see you're okay. I'm going to need a statement—"

"You can take a formal statement after he's had a meal and some rest," Dr. Sinclair said firmly.

Mr. Graham looked at Tor, who took another huge bite of his turkey sandwich.

"How about coffee and sweet rolls?" Grandma Douglas chirped. "I want to hear the rest of Tor's story."

Mr. Graham sighed and took a seat in a chair. He looked exhausted. "We found evidence of foul play in the death of the Slader boy," he said. "We'd just opened the investigation when Ms. Adams's husband, Joe, called me. I spent the night up here looking for you. I thought you were dead, and you show up alive and hand me the killer."

"You're welcome," Tor said through his mouthful of sandwich. He wasn't sure what he was supposed to say.

"I'll tell you what," Mr. Graham said. Everyone leaned forward. "I'll take his statement in a few hours, after he's had some rest."

"But what about us?" Grandma Douglas wailed.

"Well, he can talk while he's resting," the CBI man murmured, looking out the window and scratching his chin. "That is, if he wants to."

"I want to," Tor said. He noticed Mr. Graham fiddling with his shirt pocket after he scratched his chin, and he thought perhaps Mr. Graham had a recording device in that pocket. He didn't mind. He wasn't trying to keep a lie straight; he was simply going to tell the truth.

He talked himself hoarse, while Mrs. Douglas and Grandma served coffee and a sweet sticky pastry, while Sheriff Hartman wrote busily, and Mr. Graham finished his pastry and then rolled a toothpick slowly from one corner of his mouth to the other. The mayor sat quietly with his hands folded over his big belly.

Tor tried to explain how he'd been so happy to make it through the trees that he wasn't aware he was in the White Gates, and how he'd figured out too late that Jeff and Max were screaming at him to stop.

"They said 'stop'?" Sheriff Hartman asked, raising his head from his notes.

"They tried to stop me," Tor said. "They really did. I don't think they meant to chase me into the White Gates, and I know they didn't mean to set off the avalanche."

"My boy," Mayor Malone said huskily. He cleared his throat, but said nothing else.

"We know they were trying to save you, Tor," Dr. Sinclair said. "They told everyone where you were so we could search for you."

"They might tell you about the blood doping, too," Tor said. "If you ask them, I mean. I don't think they knew that's why Brian died. Deputy Rollins, he—"

"Just plain Rollins, if you please," Sheriff Hartman said.

"Rollins, I think he talked them into blood doping," Tor said. "I don't think they knew Brian died from the blood doping. They thought his death was my mom's fault, and Rollins, he wanted them to believe that, too. They were mean because they were scared, that's what I think."

"That doesn't excuse their behavior," Ms. Adams said sternly. "They knew what they were doing. They knew it was wrong."

"Your son never told you about the blood doping, sir?" the sheriff asked.

"Not a word," the mayor said heavily.

"They'll be quite a help, I think, now that they know the truth," Mr. Graham said through his toothpick. "You went through this . . . gate?"

"Over a cliff," Tor said with satisfaction. "But the snow was so deep I didn't get hurt. I was stuck in the snow for a bit until I worked my way loose. Then I heard the avalanche siren and felt the rumbling."

Dr. Sinclair gripped the edge of the desk as Tor explained how he'd scooted back to the cliff, trying to shelter in the rocks, and had seen a dark space that might hold him. When he explained about the avalanche crushing the tree to bits, everyone leaned forward intently, hanging on his every word. It was very gratifying.

"I found Raine's flashlight in my pocket," Tor said. "From . . . from walking home the other night." He'd almost said when they'd broken into the mayor's office.

"My flashlight!" Raine gasped, and gave a little sigh. "I'd forgotten you still had it."

"Lucky I did," Tor said. He could feel a surf of exhaustion rolling toward him, cresting like an ocean wave coming into shore. Not all the tea or sandwiches in the world were going to keep him awake much longer, but he had to keep talking. The best part was coming up.

"I walked for what seemed like forever through the tunnels. Then I found a lantern, and matches," he said, and took a deep breath. "They were sitting right next to your great-great-great-grandma, Raine."

His words fell into a silence as deep as a well, as deep as the silence in the tunnel. Even Mr. Graham had stopped rolling his toothpick, and his mother and Ms. Adams looked like statues on either side of the desk.

"Leaping Water?" Raine whispered.

"Yeah," Tor said, and reached inside his jacket. "She gave me this, Raine. For your family. She was waiting for me."

"Waiting for you," Sheriff Hartman said in a blank sort of way. He wasn't writing anything down; his pencil was held in the air like he'd forgotten he was holding it.

"Yeah, for me. The healer's son. She wanted me to break the curse, of course," Tor said impatiently. He held out the envelope to Raine. "This belongs to your family. We have to protect her people now. That's our job now."

"It's the deed to the mountain," Raine said in a tiny voice. She handed the envelope to her father, who looked at it as though he'd forgotten how to read. He held it out to his wife, who passed it to Grandma Douglas. Grandma Douglas held it to her chest and bowed her ancient head.

"That's the original deed?" Mayor Malone asked. He sounded wheezy, like he'd been hit in the stomach.

"What is the significance of this?" Mr. Graham asked. He looked both puzzled and irritated. "What is this?"

"This is the deed to the Borsh Mountain land," Mr. Douglas said, taking the envelope from Grandma Douglas and holding it carefully in both hands. "This is the proof that my family needs to keep the development from going forward on our mountain."

"Or you can sell the mountain and keep the money for your family," Mayor Malone said desperately. "There's that. There's a lot of money—"

"No," Tor, Drake, and Raine said as one. Everyone turned to look at them.

"We have to protect our people," Raine said proudly, her chin up. "That is what Leaping Water did. That's why she gave the deed to Tor. That is our duty now."

"Tor found a skeleton in a tunnel," Mayor Malone said. "That's what he found. Talking about protecting some mythical people, that's crazy talk. You'll want to think this over, Mr. Douglas. That's a lot of money we're talking about there."

"Thank you, sir," Mr. Douglas said gently, and tucked the envelope in his shirt. "I'll certainly consider it."

"What does this have to do with Brian Slader and blood doping?" asked Mr. Graham impatiently.

"Nothing, and everything," Tor said. "The curse on the town is what Deputy—er, Mr.—Rollins used to keep the blood doping a secret, even after Brian died. That's why the snowboarders chased me out of bounds. That's why Jeff and Max tried to knock me down and instead I ended up in the White Gates. They believed Brian died because of the curse. It all happened because of the curse."

"What curse?" asked Mr. Graham, and Tor sat back for a bit while the room erupted in noise and explanation. The warmth of Drake against one side of him and Raine on the other was so comforting that Tor actually began to doze off.

"Tor, don't fall asleep," Ms. Adams said, and Tor snapped awake to see that everyone was looking at him again.

"I'm awake," he insisted, though all the angles of the room seemed to be bent in strange ways. He blinked. "What?"

"How did you get out?" Sheriff Hartman said.

"The light, in the morning," Tor said. "The light and the breeze down the passageway. I found the crack in the wall and kicked my way through. Then I saw the gray wall and the ladder."

He laughed, because it seemed so funny now, and rolled his head on the couch to look first at Raine, then at Drake. His head was much too heavy to lift now.

"I thought maybe I was dead, the room was so white and strange and there was the silver ladder right up to heaven, but it turned out to be the ladder on the chairlift pylon. There was a hatch at the top, and I came out to see that I was back on the mountain. The rest, you know," he said tiredly, and closed his eyes again.

"The construction crew must have blocked up the mine tunnel when they dug the chairlift pylon," Mayor Malone said.

"That was the way out," Dr. Sinclair said. "He found the way out."

"Kicked my way out, really," Tor mumbled.

"Well done, son," Mr. Douglas said, and Tor could have sworn he was close to tears.

"Yes, well done," Ms. Adams said, and he was sure she was crying.

"Oh, it wasn't really me," Tor said at the very edge of sleep. "Not me. Drake and Raine and me. It was us."

"Yeah," Raine whispered. Drake made an embarrassed shrugging movement that jostled Tor and reminded him of something. He turned his head to Drake and it seemed to take forever as the room slowly rotated and Drake came into view.

"I never saw anything like that jump you made when you made Deputy Rollins crash," Tor mumbled. "You think you could teach me that move?"

"Yes," Drake said, "I will." That was the last thing Tor remembered. He dreamed of otters, and Leaping Water, and bells that rang like music in the darkness.

17 ☠ BLESSING

THE CHAIRLIFTS STOOD silent now, their shadows making black squares over the brilliant emerald grass of the empty mountain. The snow was gone and so, too, were the crowds of skiers and snowboarders. The pine trees were almost black in the hot sun. Their trunks were cloaked in shadow and their branches were a perfect dark velvet green. The air was alive with butterflies and bees and motes of pollen and the excited chatter of birds and squirrels.

Tor stopped for a moment and took out his water bottle. It felt strange to be wearing shorts and a T-shirt again, to feel the air lifting the hair from his forehead and brushing against his arms and bare legs.

"Drake, stop," Raine called. Drake was walking ahead and hadn't seen Tor stop. Drake had given up his horrible winter sweaters, but his summer wardrobe included shorts in the most awful patterns Tor had ever seen. Today he was wearing neon orange and green plaid golf shorts. He turned, and then came back toward them, jumping like a goat down the slope.

"Water break," Dr. Sinclair said. She wore shorts and a bucket-shaped hat that made her look hardly older than Raine. Her face was pink with exertion. "Is this where we head into the woods?"

"Not quite," Raine said. "Just a bit further up."

"Then let's rest for a minute," Dr. Sinclair said. She turned and sat down on the grass, sitting with her knees up and her elbows resting just like a snowboarder. Drake shrugged and sat down, obviously bursting with energy and wishing they would go on. Tor and Raine sat down next to Dr. Sinclair. The four of them contemplated the valley and the town of Snow Park, laid out like a tiny miniature toy town below them.

"It's pretty from up here," Dr. Sinclair said, sipping from her bottle. She turned her face up to the sun and gave a sigh of happiness.

Tor looked down toward home, planting his elbows on the warm springy grass. It seemed like he'd been here all his life.

Raine tilted her head back like Dr. Sinclair and closed her eyes, smiling into the sun. Water beaded her face. Her hair was braided as always but she'd taken to wearing Ute beading in the loops that tied off the ends, and she'd sewn tiny beads in a pattern along the sides of her shorts. She didn't mind being a Ute anymore, Tor thought.

"Come *on*, let's go already," Drake said.

Tor got to his feet as Drake bounced impatiently in his plaid shorts. Raine flipped her braids over her shoulders, Dr. Sinclair pulled down her bucket hat, and they turned upslope and began to walk.

The slope got steeper and more slippery as they walked steadily on. Finally they were at the top of the White Gates. Without snow they looked like stony scars on the mountain. Dr. Sinclair stood for a long moment looking down the avalanche chute, her eyes stricken, and then she turned to Tor with a shrug as if to say "I'm a mom, I can't help it," and followed Drake and Raine into the woods.

"The judge was so eager to give us the land," Raine said as the trees closed around them. "I didn't think it would be so easy."

"I think the judge was looking for an excuse to give the land back to you," Dr. Sinclair said gently. "Guilt, I suppose."

"And he wasn't a snowboarder," Drake said.

"Oh, Drake," Raine laughed, and threw a pinecone at him.

"That's your pinecone," Tor said. He picked up another one and chucked it at Drake. "Here's another pinecone. Yours, all yours. We can throw them at Drake all day."

"Oh, Tor, you don't get it, do you?" Raine said. She let her fingers trail down the branches of a tree. It gave under her touch and then sprang back up again after she passed. The pine smell was strong in the air. "I don't think of this land as mine, or yours, or anyone's. This mountain doesn't belong to anybody. It belongs to itself, and it always will."

"What is this, a poem?" Drake asked.

"I don't care if it sounds silly," Raine said, flipping her braids over her shoulder and glaring at Drake. "If we have to 'own' this land to protect it, then I'm happy to own it. But we know whose land this really is."

"The river people," Tor said, and the breeze came through the pines and set the tops dancing. He laughed and swung his arms wide and spun in a circle.

Drake clapped a hand to his head. "I'm going to retch," he said.

"Say it," Raine said, and picked up a broken branch. She poked at Drake with it, and he jumped. "Say it, say the river people own this all."

She chased him in a circle around Tor and his mother. Dr. Sinclair stood with her hands on her hips, shaking her head, and Drake finally threw up his hands as Raine stopped, panting, and made as if to throw the branch at him.

"The river people, the river people!" he shouted, and Tor could hear the echo through the trunks of the pines. "This all belongs to the river people! There, you satisfied?"

"Mostly," Raine said, throwing down the branch and panting. Drake was fast. "Just one more thing to do, and that's Dr. Sinclair's job."

"Ah, yes, my task in this little jaunt," Dr. Sinclair said. "Anyone going to tell me what it is yet? Anyone going to fill me in on why I'm up here and who these mysterious river people are?"

"Soon," Tor promised. "While we're young, Raine?"

Raine waved her hand in a come-on gesture and they set off through the woods, angling deeper into the mountain. The hike was a lot longer on foot than it was gliding on a snowboard. They took another water break in a small clearing that was so dense with trees that Tor started to feel chilled in the shade. When they stepped into the sun again, he turned his face up to it and nearly killed himself stumbling over a log, which made Drake laugh heartily. Tor chucked a pinecone and hit Drake in the seat of his neon plaid shorts. Drake yelped and started to chase Tor, but Dr. Sinclair made them stop.

After they had continued walking for so long that Tor thought they'd gone the wrong way, he recognized the clearing in the trees ahead of them.

"Quiet," Raine commanded, and they stopped. She stood for a moment, listening intently. Tor could hear the gurgle of water and the sigh of the breeze through the pine trees, and nothing else. Raine waved them on and they flitted like ghosts through the trees and came out on the small bluff overlooking the valley where the otters lived.

The valley was alive with water. Multiple creeks chuckled and gurgled, joining a larger river that roared white as it disappeared out of the lower end of the valley. The sunlight was warm and full and the beaver ponds in the center of the valley glowed like blue jewels. Green grasses and spiky willow bushes lined the creeks and covered a marshy area. Tall aspen groves were still unfurling their pale green leaves.

"This is beautiful," Dr. Sinclair whispered. They sat down at the edge of the bluff and Tor looked eagerly up and down the valley, seeking the sleek brown heads of the otters.

There was nothing. Birds flew in and out of the willow trees and there was a low and sleepy hum of insects, but nothing else moved. Tor shifted a little and Raine laid a warm brown hand on his arm.

"Peace," she said in a whisper so low he almost didn't hear her. Then he did, and he felt something inside him come completely unknotted. Whatever happened wasn't up to him. For the first time he really understood what Raine meant when she said she didn't own this land. He didn't own it either, and he didn't own the otters. They weren't going to appear just to entertain him, because they weren't his.

Tor didn't know how long they sat there. The sun soaked into him and the sleepy hum filled him up. Dr. Sinclair was calm and still, moving only to breathe and to take a drink from her water bottle now and again. Maybe she, too, felt the timelessness of this place. Tor glanced at her and she was smiling gently.

Drake tensed, and Tor saw the first of the brown heads break the water. He sighed and heard Drake and Raine sigh with him as an otter poured itself onto the land and stood looking around, eyes like black oil, whiskers twitching. A second otter tumbled out of the water and the two rubbed noses, then a third otter splashed to the shore.

Dr. Sinclair didn't move. She sat still, her eyes on the otters. Tor could see the knowledge in her face, the comprehension. She knew what she was seeing. She drew a deep, slow breath.

"The river people," she breathed out, and Tor, Drake, and Raine nodded as one.

There was a long silence then, as they watched the otters play on the riverbank. They were a beautiful glossy brown in the summer sunlight. Their ears and tails were black and their noses were like a dog's, with a short snout and a black button nose. They seemed to relish rubbing noses, sliding their bodies over one another, and using their broad, powerful tails to flip water at each other like children having a water fight.

Dr. Sinclair finally sat up straight, slowly, and put her hands out, palms up.

"I promise," she said clearly, in a normal tone of voice. At her voice the otters looked up sharply and froze. "I promise to guard you. I promise to keep your secret. I make this promise to Leaping Water and her family. I make this promise to you."

A moment later the otters were gone, sliding into the water with incredible speed and leaving not a single splash behind. Dr. Sinclair sat for a moment longer with her hands out, and then she dropped her hands and looked over at Drake and Raine, then at Tor, with a rueful smile.

"I hope I didn't scare them away for good," she whispered.

"No, I don't think you did," Raine said with shining eyes. "I don't think you did."

"Was that right?" Dr. Sinclair whispered. "Was that what I should have said?"

"That was exactly right," Drake whispered.

Tor reached out and took Raine's hand. She reached out and took Drake's hand, and Tor felt his mother take his. They sat with hands clasped. Tor felt roots growing deep inside of him, roots growing into the warm earth.

"There they are," Raine breathed, as the otter heads broke the surface of the stream. The second otter made a squeaking cry, glanced up at the four of them, and turned away, dismissing them.

That was when the first of the baby otters appeared.

☠AFTERWORD

Dear Reader,

Thank you for visiting Torin Sinclair's new hometown of Snow Park. Now that you know the secret of Leaping Water's people, I'd like to share my own encounter with wild Colorado river otters.

A few summers ago, my family took a hike deep into the Rocky Mountains. We were fishing along a river when my little daughter slipped and fell into the icy water. We plucked her out quickly but she was already shivering.

The rest of the family hiked upriver while I dried my daughter off and warmed her up. We were sitting quietly on a rock in the sunshine, wrapped in my jacket and cuddled close, when an otter popped up in the water and scrambled onto a rock across the stream. We sat, barely breathing, while the otter warmed up on its sunny rock.

When the rest of the family returned, the otter disappeared. I made everyone sit and wait for what seemed like forever. I began to think we had imagined the otter. Then everyone gasped because we realized that an entire otter family was watching us from the far bank. The otter had gone home to collect its family so they could see these odd two-legged creatures. We stared at each other for a long time, and I don't know who was more fascinated, the otters or us.

This magical river doesn't belong to my family. It belongs to the otters and other wild creatures, because in America we've decided to protect our most beautiful places and keep them free. These places, including our many national parks and forests, are treasures that we've agreed to keep for each other. Encounters like the one my family had with the otters can be moving reminders of why this is so important.

—Bonnie Ramthun